My Sweet Lisa

Anne Louise Bannon

HH
Healcroft House, Publishers
Altadena, California

ISBN 978-1-948616-23-2
Library of Congress Control Number: 2022903473

Contents

To Michael

Acknowledgments

How do I thank the many, many people who provide love, support, and information to me?

First up, I have to thank Paula Bernstein, MD, PhD, who answered my endless questions and is still a good friend.

Then there are the wonderful folks at the Repair Café who are getting used to the idea that talking to me is going be... um... different.

And, finally, the many support and marketing groups that I work with, including the Lady Sings the Clues author pod, the Blackbird Writers, and Sisters in Crime. It doesn't get any better.

March 21, 1985

.

M y eyes blurred as I looked at yet another article on Ivan Danschenko, a nice importer of Russian goods and known KGB operative. He was supposedly meeting with Sid down in Westwood Village while I looked up articles on the microfilm reader in the UCLA library. Sid and I had sold an article to one of the major business magazines on Russian immigrants working on building businesses here in the U.S., but it was also our cover for checking into Danschenko.

"Sid, this can't possibly work. She's got to be onto us."
"Don't worry, Frank. It will."

Sid Hackbirn, and I, Lisa Wycherly, are not just freelance writers. Within the structures of the FBI and CIA are several organizations so top secret that people don't know they even exist. Sid and I belong to one called Operation Quickline, which is under the FBI. We usually do courier work. But someone in the CIA had decided that the last thing The Company needed was an agent that the Soviets might be able to track to check up on some known KGB operatives who were supposedly trying to defect. The Company was what we called the CIA when we weren't using ruder terms. Henry James, our immediate supervisor for Quickline, had asked us to take the job on, warning us that Danschenko was not only trying to defect, he'd been working as a double agent, as well. So, since I usually take on the background research and Sid does the interviews (he's a lot better at those than I am), I was stuck in the library on a rainy day making my eyes water staring at the microfilm reader.

It was my birthday, too. Sid and I had celebrated the night before because Sid was concerned that the interview might run long and Danschenko had insisted on scheduling it for late the afternoon of my birthday. That Saturday, we were going to celebrate again with my sister and her family in Fullerton.

"Calm down, Frank. She won't show early. I told her six-thirty and that's when she'll be here.

"You gave it away? She'll know something's up."

"She doesn't suspect a thing. I took her out last night, even gave her a present. She probably thinks I have a tight connection with a stewardess."

I glared at the microfilm reader. There was no hint in the article that Danschenko was anything other than what he claimed to be, namely a nice guy who ran an import business and was attempting to claim his share of "The American Dream." Which was rather annoying, not so much because I wanted to believe that Danschenko was a bad guy, but because I felt like I was spinning my wheels researching him. At least, I'd gotten one of the readers that also printed. I checked to see how much change I had left. I was running low. I printed the article, anyway. My purse already bulged with a ton of other copies I'd made, not only on Danschenko, but several other Russian businesspeople.

"Sid, who are all these people?"

"Mae, I'm not entirely sure. The teens are from the church youth group. Some of the others are from that Singles Bible Study. Henry, Lydia, and Angelique are friends of ours through our writing. The rest, Frank and Esther found, and I have no idea."

Sid used to be my boss. That winter, we'd formed a business partnership because as Sid put it, we were, in fact, a team. He'd hired me as his secretary, originally, and that's how most people know us. I did not know he had recruited me into his espionage business until it was too late, but I hadn't minded as much as you might think. I got a decided kick out of being a spy.

Sid's not a large man, only about three inches taller than me, and I'm average height. But he is, well, gorgeous, with dark, wavy hair, intense blue eyes, and a cleft chin.

I also live in his house, which does give rise to all sorts of rumors, although Sid and I aren't... Well, you know. Sid was known for being loose as the proverbial goose, and me, I'm still a virgin. We simply have different values is all. Sid was raised to believe in free love. I was raised to believe that sex belongs to the marital state. We were having a few problems that way, but the relationship that we'd built over the time we'd been working together was still better than being without each other.

"Think she'll be surprised, Dad?"
"I'm sure she will, Nick."

I scuffed the toe of my armored running shoes against the table leg. They were black running shoes with a screwdriver, wires, spring steel to pick locks and other stuff hidden in the soles. I also wore an older pair of jeans and a pink Oxford shirt. Sid had questioned my attire, pointing out that it was still business hours. I had pointedly returned that with the weather being as rainy as it was and the fact that I was going to be out way past business hours, I was darned well going to be comfortable. I checked my watch again. 6:05. It was close enough. Sid had asked me to meet him at a nice little Italian restaurant that we both liked in the Village. It would be tight, but I figured I could probably get my car from the university parking lot, then get a new space not far from the restaurant in time to get there at six-thirty.

"This is never going to work."
"In the first place, Frank, it was your brilliant idea that it would. And in the second place, the only person who could have given it away is you."

I drove past the restaurant. I saw Sid standing in front, just beyond where a black van sat at the curb. I parked my truck in a nearby lot and decided to leave my purse in the car. The rain had stopped, but I still picked up my raincoat. I hurried around the corner, idly noticing that the van had, apparently, already gone around the block, and was getting ready to drive past the restaurant again.

Sid saw me and grinned. When he got close enough, he took my hands and gave me a quick kiss.

"Not that I'm complaining, but what's that for?" I asked, my eyes following the van.

Sid's eyes followed, as well. "Just felt like it." He paused. "You saw the van, too."

"Yeah. It's probably nothing."

"Probably." His smile returned. "Did you get any good stuff?"

"That's why my purse is in my truck, but it's pretty benign. I'd suspect some of the other guys you're interviewing sooner than I would Danschenko, based on what I've read. You get anything?"

He led me into the restaurant. "Not really. Come on. I've got us a private room."

"Why?"

"It's your birthday."

"We celebrated last night."

He grinned. "Why not celebrate again?"

He pushed me toward the door and opened it.

The next thing I knew, I was jumping out of my skin. A whole crowd of people screamed "Surprise!" and "Happy birthday!"

"Oh, my god," I gasped, backing into Sid. "What on earth...?"

"Happy birthday, Lisa!" Frank Lonnergan, my dear friend gave me a big hug. "This is your birthday party."

"What?" I looked over at Sid, who grinned.

"It was a team effort," Sid said. He was perfect, as always, in a three-piece suit and pin under the knot of his tie.

"Exactly!" hollered Esther Nguyen. "You can't take all the credit, Frank. We deserve some!"

Kathy Deiner and her fiancé, Jesse White, just grinned as I screamed when I saw my sister, Mae, and her husband, Neil.

"And you brought the kids!" I yelped as I went to hug my nieces and nephews. "And Nick! Oh, I'm so glad you're here, sweetie!"

Nick, who was then twelve, is Sid's belatedly discovered son, and a dead ringer for his father, even with his glasses. Sid and I had barely known him a year, but he'd become so very close to us. I gave him a big hug, then looked around the room.

"Who else is here?" I asked, then yelped as I saw my friend and confessor, Father John, who smiled quietly and backed off.

"That's what we'd like to know," said Mae.

"You're telling me," said Frank. "Your address book is a mess."

"You raided my address book?" I couldn't help glaring at him.

"We had to," said Sid. "Half your friends wouldn't be here otherwise. Good gravy, woman, you should have told us what all you're up to."

"I agree," said Mae, with a grin. "I didn't know you were a Eucharistic Minister."

I blushed. "Darby did. He went with me a couple times to deliver the Sacrament."

My eyes filled as I realized that the four old women and two old men who I visited as many Sundays as I could were scattered about the room.

Sid and Frank had done their work well. There were three friends from the St. Vincent de Paul Society, several from the Friends of the Los Angeles Public Library, Marlene Ramsey and Karen Jones from the racquetball club. Sid's and my friend Henry James was there with his wife, Lydia. Most people knew Henry as Sid's contact for a regular column on the FBI. Henry was the Public Information Officer for the Los Angeles office. Sid and I had both gotten rather attached to him and Lydia. But then, there was also Angelique Carter, who was Henry's secretary. She had been one of Sid's more regular girlfriends, but I had good reason to believe that was no longer the case.

I gasped when I saw my friend Rick there. He was standing, but just barely. His cheeks had sunken in and there were deep bags under his eyes. He smiled, nonetheless.

"Rick, you came." I hugged him.

He nodded. "I had to. I just won't be able to stay long."

Rick was dying of AIDS.

"That you're here at all is wonderful," I told him.

"Even the Dragon has sent her regards," Sid whispered to me.

The Dragon was probably one of the top agents in Quick-line.

"Really?" I asked him.

He shrugged. "I also have a telegram from Marian and An-drew."

"You have got to be kidding," I said.

Marian and Andrew were a couple of British CID agents that Sid and I had come across.

Sid held up his hands in wonderment. But it didn't matter. I shortly found myself at a table in the back corner of the room with any number of delicious things to eat in front of me. Sid, despite his healthy eating habit, refrained from lecturing me about what I was doing to my insides. [Oh, come on. It was your birthday. I wasn't that inflexible. - SEH]

Father John led us all in a quick grace, then the party really took off. After we'd mostly eaten, Frank insisted that I kiss all the males in the room. Charlie Fields, one of the teens, got in line twice. I heard Sid chuckling after I kissed Mr. Ramon, one of my old men.

"What?" I asked.

Sid snickered. "You did a lot for the old guy. I hope I'm in as good a shape when I'm his age."

"You reprobate."

Sid just laughed.

Neil and Father John got brotherly pecks on the cheek. My youngest nephews, twins Marty and Mitch, who were four, both wiped their kisses off. I laughed. They would have been furious if I'd left them out.

I saved Frank and Sid for the last. Frank dipped me. Sid gently placed his hand on my cheek and caressed my lips with his. I loved him so much, which was kind of a problem. He couldn't say the words and he couldn't promise to be faithful sexually to me. But neither of us could handle being without the other. I pulled away, blushing, as a chorus of catcalls broke out. He chuckled.

Time slipped by. My seniors left early, although Mrs. Salcido made a point of giving me a big hug from her wheelchair, then pointed at Sid.

"You," she commanded. "You be sure to marry this girl. She deserves someone good."

I flushed and Sid chuckled nervously. Father John coughed as if he were holding in his laughter. It was one of those things that would have been awkward under the best of circumstances, but was made worse because of... Well, let's just say the whole marriage thing had gotten to be a sore point.

Sid recovered first. "I'll see what I can do."

"I'm sorry, Sid," I hissed at him a moment later. "I'm sure she didn't know."

[Like hell, the old bat didn't. - SEH]

"It's okay," he said softly. "It's bound to come up."

It was getting to be ten o'clock. My almost seven-year-old niece Ellen had fallen asleep in one of the booths, and Marty and Mitch were getting cranky. Mae's older two, Darby and Janey, were looking a little dopey-eyed, as well. Several of the teens had left. We moved out of the room to the street. Neil took off to get the family car while Sid held Ellen, still sound asleep, and chatted with Mae. Mae's kids all adore Uncle Sid. Frank and Esther were still in the room, rounding up all the gaily wrapped presents that people had brought.

I held my raincoat and chatted pleasantly with one of the new teens, Eliana Martinez. She was a sweet young woman, about sixteen. She'd only moved to the U.S. from Colombia in January. She and her mother were living with her aunt not far from Sid and me in Beverly Hills. The two of us had bonded because I could see that she was carrying some sort of secret, and I certainly knew what that felt like. Jesse White stood nearby talking to someone else.

Out of the corner of my eye, I saw a black van, possibly the one Sid and I had seen earlier, pull up. I smiled, but all my senses were on alert. Three men in black fatigues and masks burst out of the back of the van. I screamed, and so did several other people. I also put myself between them and Eliana.

After that, I knew no more.

March 21–22, 1985

Sid's Voice

That fucking black van.

I saw it pull up. I knew Lisa had seen it, too.

Ninety-nine times out of a hundred, you see stuff like that, it's nothing. Absolutely nothing. Lisa and I notice because we do see that one time out of a hundred that it's something bad.

I shoved Ellen at Mae as I saw the men burst out of the van. Lisa did exactly what I would have expected her to do. She put Eliana Martinez behind her and screamed her head off. I was surprised to see Jesse pull Eliana even further away and reach after Lisa. It didn't help. The men grabbed Lisa. One put a cloth to her nose, and a second later, they were gone, the van somehow roaring away through the Westwood traffic. Lisa's raincoat lay on the ground.

Eliana sank to the sidewalk, sobbing. Jesse bent over her, then looked up at me.

"I'm sorry, Sid," he gasped. "I tried to get her. I couldn't."

"You did your best," I said. I could feel my voice, dull and blank.

John Reynolds put his hand on my shoulder. "I don't know if it's any comfort to you, but she's in God's hands now."

Henry was there, too. Being official law enforcement, he took over, making sure that all the witnesses remained close at hand. Lydia, Henry's wife, led me to one of the chairs lined up outside the restaurant door for people waiting for tables. Mae was already seated there, and Lydia sat me next to her. The children were now wide awake and trembling and Mae held the twins and Ellen in her lap. Darby sat on her other side. Janey, who was eight, slid up to me. I wasn't surprised. Janey and I... Well, she was special. I choked. Not unlike how special Lisa was.

"It'll be alright, Uncle Sid," she said softly.

"Thanks, Janey." I returned the sweet hug.

Neil showed up a minute later. He and Mae had a quick conference. The kids protested, but Neil took them home and left Mae, who sat back down next to me. Nick showed up at my other side and sat down.

"Dad?" he asked.

"I'm here, Nick." I wasn't, but what else was there to say? I held him close.

Angelique Carter, who was Henry's secretary, came up with Lisa's raincoat and gave it to me.

"They're going to do everything they can, Sid," she said softly. She hesitated a moment, then bent and hugged me tightly.

I held her back and debated asking her to stay, but she slid away before I could, and I realized that I didn't really want her to, at least, not in my bedroom. Yeah, Ange and I had that kind of relationship. Or we'd had. It had been months since we'd last had sex with each other and I'd heard she'd dropped out of the singles scene. Lisa and she were both very good friends.

The police were there and several others. I was past noticing at that point. I answered what questions I could and gave the cops the license plate on the van. John managed to tell me that there was a group going to their church to say mass. I was glad. That was exactly the sort of thing Lisa would appreciate. John invited me to join them, and I shook my head.

"We have to find Lisa's truck," I told Mae at some point.

As soon as the police let us, I headed toward the nearest parking structure with Mae and Nick at my side.

"Can you drive a manual transmission back to our place?" I asked Mae.

"I haven't in a while, but I could." Mae, however, looked more skeptical than not.

I sighed and got the key to Lisa's truck out of my key case.

"We'll find my car first, then, and you can drive that to the house." I handed her the key case and Lisa's raincoat. "That's the key to my Beemer and that's the house key. Take Nick with you."

"Dad!" Nick groaned.

"It'll be alright, Nick," Mae said.

Given that we were in Westwood, Lisa's dark blue Datsun pickup could have been anywhere, but somehow it turned up in the same structure I'd parked my BMW, even on the same floor. I saw the truck and squeezed my eyes shut.

"Sid," Mae said, putting her hand on my shoulder. "She's going to be okay."

I looked at her. "You don't know that."

"No. But I have to believe it."

We went over to my car and Mae got it open.

"Nick, will you show Aunt Mae the other guest room?" I asked.

"Can't I ride with you?" he asked, plaintively.

"No. I'd rather take Lisa's truck by myself."

"I'll see you at the house," Mae said, helping Nick into the front passenger seat.

"Yeah." I looked away. "Don't wait up."

Mae put her hand on my arm. "Sid, where are you going?"

"To get laid."

Nick looked like he was about to burst into tears. I felt like shit leaving him like that but didn't know what else to do. I waited while Mae got my car going. Then I left the structure.

The bar wasn't far and in the cool of the night air, the walk felt good. Inside, the haze of cigarette smoke was breathably thin. I surveyed the occupants. Two possibles sitting at the bar, another in a booth alone. I chose her.

Bourbon and water in hand, I headed for the booth. It was time. Play the game, get a conversation going, get into bed. Anything for the release I so desperately needed. It was what I knew. It was what I did.

"I notice you're alone." I forced the smile onto my face.

She was a shapely blond, although her eyes were dark and somewhat small. I really liked Lisa's big, round eyes.

"More or less," she said. "I could be looking for some company."

"So could I." I slid into the booth next to her.

She wore standard Dress for Success, although the bow on her blouse had been undone. Her fingernails were short and painted in a dark color, which meant she worked in a business context, but probably in a clerical capacity.

"So, how do you like secretarial work?" I asked.

She laughed. "How did you know I'm a secretary?"

"Observation and deduction."

"Oh, I get it." She giggled, damn her. "You're one of those fancy detectives."

"Not quite." I sipped my drink.

"What do you do for a living?"

"As little as possible."

The same flip line had slipped out before I could stop it. The night I'd met Lisa, she'd asked the same thing and had not been amused by my response. At the time, I'd put it down to the fact that she'd been out of work for a year. I'd had no idea then that Lisa's tolerance for bullshit was pretty low, in general. As we'd grown to know each other, her tolerance for my bullshit morphed into no tolerance for it at all. She could be more forgiving of others.

The blond grinned. "So, what are you doing the rest of the night?"

I tried to smile but couldn't. I didn't feel any of the usual stirrings. If anything, my gut clenched. I put my glass on the table and left. I didn't hear what the blond shouted after me, but didn't really care, either.

I didn't even go into the next bar. I tried to think of how it would feel. Instead, my mind filled with the soft curves of Lisa's breasts, her hips, her round eyes gazing at me. Her high school class ring all but burned in my right pants pocket.

I could not understand what was happening to me, but the thought of another woman sickened me.

I pulled the white gold ring with the light blue stone out of my pocket and slid it onto the little finger of my right hand. She'd called it reassurance when she'd given it to me after I'd given her my high school ring. I am not one for superstition, but I knew her ring was not coming off my hand until Lisa was safe in my arms again, and maybe not even after that. I twisted it a couple times, then walked back to where her truck was parked.

It was midnight when I got home. I briefly debated going to bed, but I knew sleep would not come. I went into the library. I shouldn't have. It was one of Lisa's favorite rooms in the house, even though it was mostly given over to my ebony baby grand piano. Lisa had made the pillows on the burgundy velvet wing back chairs. Her books were mixed in with mine, although I was the one who had organized them the previous fall. The music rack next to the piano overflowed with sheet music that Lisa had bought. I sat down at the keys of the piano, not needing the sheet music for Chopin's Prelude Number Fifteen. It was Lisa's favorite.

I only got a few bars in when it all overwhelmed me. The tears came slowly. I don't cry easily. But there was nothing else to do.

"Dad?" Nick's voice came from the door.

He was wearing his pajamas, but clearly had not been able to sleep, either.

"Oh. Hi," I said.

"You're crying." He came over and sat on the piano bench next to me.

"Yeah." I wiped the tears from my face.

"I've been crying, too." He leaned next to me and pushed his glasses up on his nose. "Dad, what's going to happen to Lisa?"

That was the last thing I wanted to think about.

"I don't know, Nick," I said. "The FBI and the police are working on it. I was able to give them the license plate on the van. But that's all."

"I'm scared."

"So, am I."

"Dad, can I stay here 'til they find Lisa? I think Mom would be happier if I was here, anyway. Can I?"

"Sure, Nick. I'd like that."

"Dad, why can't I live with you?"

I squeezed my eyes shut. The truth was, I really did want Nick to live with us, with Lisa and me. But there was Quickline. I couldn't tell him about that, and it wasn't a safe environment for him. How had Lisa explained it to Jesse and Kathy when they'd confronted us?

"Nick, there is a really good reason why you can't right now. The problem is, I can't tell you what it is. You'll just have to trust me that it's a really good reason, and if it weren't for that, I would have you living with us right now."

"Okay." Nick looked downcast but hugged me anyway.

And, at last, I found the release, the comfort I'd been looking for. I hugged him back.

"I love you, Dad."

"I love you, Nick."

How the hell was I able to say it? I definitely meant it. I loved Nick almost as much as... That was the problem. I couldn't say the same to Lisa. I'd known her longer and there was no question she meant more to me than anyone had. Hell, if Lisa hadn't been there when Rachel, Nick's mom, had dumped him on me, I would not have had a relationship with my son.

"Dad, I don't want to sleep by myself tonight. Can I sleep with you?"

I smiled and nodded. "Sure. Why don't you?"

It would mean wearing my pajama pants. I normally slept in the raw, but somehow that didn't seem quite right with Nick there. Yet I knew having him next to me was better than having another woman.

As we slid under the covers on my waterbed, I flipped open the cover on my antique pocket watch to let the music box wind down and kept looking at it.

"Dad?" Nick asked. "Why is that watch so important?"

I closed my eyes. "Lisa gave it to me."

"Oh."

"Goodnight, Nick."

"Goodnight, Dad. Sweet dreams."

There were none. When I did sleep, my brain was filled with war and its horrors and Lisa's beautiful cow eyes looking at me in fear.

The next morning was utterly empty. The sky was overcast and threatening more rain. All I wanted to hear was Lisa's sleepy grumbling about having to run. Nick was there, as was Lisa's dog, Motley, a springer spaniel with liver-colored spots. Motley looked at me and whined as if he were asking where Lisa was.

At breakfast, Nick played with the cats. Some months before, Nick had befriended Long John Silver, a stray gray cat with one eye, and named her before we'd both found out she was a she and pregnant. The kittens, about five months old, were still in their cute phase and for all I'd talked about finding them homes, two had become permanent residents, as well. There had been four of them. Fritz, the gray tabby, was the only one I'd named, and he'd stayed with us. Lisa had named the rest. Capuchin, named after an order of monks and called Chin-Chin, and Viola had landed with Lisa's friends Kathy and Jesse. Then there was Blueberry, who was gray like her mother, but almost to the point that she looked blue.

"Nick, do you know where the pet food is?" I asked. I was vaguely aware that Lisa generally fed the cats and Motley in the morning before Conchetta, our housekeeper and cook, arrived at ten.

"Yeah. I'll get it."

Mae stumbled into the breakfast room. I caught my breath. The weird thing was that Mae and Lisa had always seemed to me to be total opposites. Mae was entirely domesticated, a full-time mom, putting her husband and kids first before everything. Lisa, on the other hand, was very career driven. Kids and family were something that she seemed to consider theoretical, as if she might be interested in them eventually, but there was too much life to explore in the meantime. While the two had similar coloring, Mae carried some padding on her figure and had a slightly rounder face. Lisa had always been skinny and her frame was well-muscled, and in spite of being six years younger than her sister, Lisa was the taller of the two. Yet, that morning, as Mae yawned and sat down at the table, all I could see was Lisa doing the same. Lisa is not a morning person.

"Sid," Mae said through sleepy eyes. "Your friend Henry, he set up a command post in your office last night. I hope that's okay."

"What?" I asked. It suddenly dawned on me that I'd seen a light in our offices the night before.

"He wants to be on top of it when the ransom demand comes through."

I nodded. That would be the appropriate procedure.

"I need to call our parents, too." Mae looked a little worried.

"No," I said. "Please don't. Your dad hates me enough as it is."

Bill Wycherly and I had achieved a level of detente about eighteen months before, but I was acutely aware of how jealous he was of me. And worried about me, with good reason I had to admit. It wasn't so much about me seducing Lisa as it was about breaking her heart. We both kind of got that we were worried about the same thing, which is probably why he hadn't tried to take me apart limb from limb. Still, it didn't mean that we were a good mix.

"He doesn't hate you," Mae said.

I rolled my eyes. "Look, can you hold off? Please? We don't have anything to tell them. If we get a ransom demand, we'll be able to figure something out."

"Mr. Hackbirn?"

The voice belonged to a tallish man with black and gray hair in a gray polyester suit. However cheap the fabric, he carried himself with authority rather than hubris.

"Yes?" I asked.

"I'm Commander Phil Reyes, LAPD. I'll be lead on this case. I'm supervising the team in your office. We need to go over the protocols."

I swallowed and nodded. "Yeah. What do I need to do?"

Reyes was professional but kind and I could see it easing Mae's anxiety. Mine? Perhaps not as much, still I was glad he was there. There wasn't much for me to understand. They would monitor all calls coming in and out. When and if the ransom demand came through, we'd discuss and formulate a plan at that time. I told them about Lisa's special code for her friends.

Lisa had set up the code back when her parents didn't know she was living in my house. Her parents would call her personal line during the day, when she was supposedly working at my place, and Lisa wouldn't pick it up because she "wasn't at home." When Lisa's friends called, they'd let it ring once, hang up, then call again. Lisa would pick up those calls. The weird thing was that even though Bill and Althea had found out where Lisa was living almost a year before, the code hung on.

As if to demonstrate, the phone rang on Lisa's line. Sure enough, the call rang once, then rang again. After getting a nod from Reyes, I picked it up.

"Sid? It's Esther."

"Hi." I had to smile. I really liked Esther Nguyen.

"Look, I know it's early, and I don't want to tie up the line, but any word yet?"

"No. It should be okay. Just use the usual signal."

"Okay. We're praying for you guys."

"Lisa would appreciate that."

"Bye."

I hung up and swallowed. Lisa believed in prayer, often teased me when things worked out in our favor, even though all I could see was chance. But that was one of the things that divided us. Faith. I had none. Hell, I was raised to be an atheist. Reyes grinned as if he was onto us and went back to the offices.

Conchetta Ramirez arrived at ten and was shocked to hear what happened. She was a medium-sized woman, in her middle forties, with strands of gray through her black hair. She had this incredible collection of concert t-shirts from mostly hard rock bands that she wore over her jeans. When she was at the house to work, she preferred to be left alone and would take both Lisa and me to task when we got in her way or got too friendly. She was our employee and did not want to be friends. Still, that morning, she patted my arm.

"This is so terrible," she said softly. "But I believe she will be all right. I know we can't say for sure. But I believe. If we all believe, that will be enough."

She patted my arm again and went off to change the sheets in the guest room. I had to admit, I was somewhat in shock. An hour later, she made a huge buffet lunch, offering some to the cops in my office.

Esther's call was just the start. A few minutes later, Kathy and Jesse dropped in to sit with me, with Frank Lonnergan right behind. John Reynolds stayed for a couple hours. Then a procession of Lisa's other friends from church came by, each saying something nice, and most of it directed at me, although they also said nice things to Mae and Nick, too. Jesse was still feeling guilty that he hadn't been able to do more to stop the kidnappers.

"You saved Eliana," Kathy finally said, looking apologetically at me.

I shut my eyes and took a deep breath. "Jesse, I saw Lisa put herself between the girl and the kidnappers. That's who Lisa is. I like to think she'd be happier knowing that Eliana, at least, was safe. And that Lisa would appreciate that."

"I failed her," Jesse said.

"So did I," I said.

Mae groaned. "Neither of you two idiots did. You both did the best you could. Sid, you were taking care of my daughter, which Lisa completely loves about you. Jesse, you took care of a sweet young woman, who, for all we know, could have been taken too. Neither of you failed Lisa. Neither of you is at fault for what happened and whining about it is only going to make it worse for all of us. Now, get over it."

Apparently, Lisa's low tolerance for bullshit was a family thing. Frank clapped Jesse on the shoulder.

"Jesse, I think Mrs. O'Malley has a point," Frank said.

Neil showed up around then with fresh clothes for Mae and the news that the kids had been farmed out.

"Janelle and Doug have the twins and Ellen," Neil told us. Mae, obviously, knew who Janelle and Doug were. "They're all pretty antsy, but Janelle swears she understands." He winced and looked at Mae apologetically. "I, uh, told everyone that Lisa had been in an accident."

"Thanks," Mae said, closing her eyes.

"Anyway, Mary Ellen Watts asked to take care of Janey, and Darby is holed up with his buddy Tad Wold."

"That's as good as we can do," Mae said.

I didn't say so but thought that Darby would have been better off with Nick. They were the same age and good friends. Neil left somewhat later. He'd taken an adjunct position at the USC dental school and had a class to teach.

"I'd cancel it, but there's going to be an opening for a full-time position next year," Neil said as I walked him out to his car. "I really want to get it. I've always liked teaching."

In addition to his regular dental practice, Neil had always taught a class at the dental school near them since I'd known him.

"What about your practice?" I asked him.

Neil shrugged. "We're trying to figure that out. I have to maintain some kind of practice, anyway, so we'll see. Just a lot of moving parts to re-arrange." He took a deep breath. "Anyway, Sid, I know we're all trying to think positive for Lisa's sake, and I'm confident we'll get her back. But I want you to know that if the worst does happen, you'll still be a part of our family. Both you and Nick."

I almost choked, it was so hard to breathe, and I was so thankful that Neil had pulled me into a firm hug because I could barely stand. It was hard enough thinking about Lisa being gone. But that Neil had the decency and the kindness to reassure me that way. I hadn't even realized I'd needed to hear it.

Somehow, I pulled myself together. "Thanks, Neil."

I watched him get into the car and drive away. Then went back inside as another car pulled up out front.

The procession of friends continued. Kathy and Jesse left in the middle of the afternoon. Frank hung on until four-thirty.

"I have to go make dinner for Esther," he told me. "Have to pay my rent somehow."

Frank is a damn fine musician. In fact, that's how the two of us bonded, initially.

Given how much luck plays into making a living in the arts and that Frank had, possibly, the worst luck of any human I've known, it was no surprise to me that Esther was, for all intents and purposes, supporting him. Esther, who was an engineer with one of the major defense plants in the area, and her father, a doctor, had bought a duplex in West Hollywood the previous fall. Around that same time, Frank had been hired for what was supposed to be a major tour with some rock star. About two cities in, however, said rock star went on a drug-induced binge for the ages, which resulted in a very well-publicized trip to rehab instead. While public sentiment was all about the poor singer's struggles, there was part of me that really resented that all the support musicians were suddenly without jobs, in particular, Frank. Fortunately for him, Esther had invited him to move in with her and her cousin.

Frank had taken the reversal of fortune in stride and was learning Vietnamese in earnest. He called it self-defense, although he'd been picking the language up here and there as long as I'd known him. Besides, Frank and Esther were not simply best buddies any more than Lisa and I were simply good friends. They joked around a lot - they both had an amazingly raucous sense of humor that belied their deep commitment to their faith - and they avoided physical affection of all kinds. But those of us who really knew them could see there was more than simple friendship between the two. It was just a matter of time. Kind of like it was for Lisa and me.

I sent Frank on his way and shut the door to the house, then went to the kitchen to see what I would do about dinner.

"I will take care of it," Conchetta snarled.

I stepped back. "But you'll have to stay late."

One of Conchetta's many boundaries was her hours. She worked from ten a.m. to five-thirty p.m., period. Her granddaughter had some medical condition – Conchetta would never elaborate on what it was – and needed specialized care. By that time, Conchetta's daughter had gotten a good day job, but the granddaughter needed to stay at a special care center, and Conchetta had to leave by five-thirty to pick the child up. Lisa and I refused to get in the way of that.

"It's alright." Conchetta glared at me, then softened a little. "I can come tomorrow, too."

"Uh." I swallowed. "That's incredibly kind of you, but no. Your family needs you and holding down the fort here will give me something to do."

She glared at me. "You better not reorganize the pantry."

I put my hands up. "I promise not to."

"I'll take care of dinner tonight and then see you Monday." She paused. "And call me if you hear anything."

"I will." I left, amazed at Conchetta's behavior.

I found myself prowling again, feeling completely mixed up. Conchetta insisting on helping past her work hours, that had filled my heart. Lisa's friends had helped, too. If only it wasn't because Lisa was in such danger.

"We're in here," Mae called from the living room.

She was sitting in one of the blue velvet wing-back chairs facing the bay window overlooking the street. Nick was nearby, playing with the cats. I sank onto the couch. Long John immediately abandoned Nick and curled up in my lap as she so often did.

"They're romancing you," Mae said.

"What? Who?"

"Lisa's friends from church. They're coming by for your sake, Sid. They've been encouraging me, too. But they're mostly coming to share their love with you."

"That's ridiculous." I shook my head. "They don't even know me that well. Not to mention that most of my dealings with that group have been extremely awkward, at best. They have no reason to love me."

"But they love Lisa, which means that's not going to stop them from loving you."

"It never stopped Lisa, either."

Suddenly, I needed to be alone. To be anywhere but there, facing what Lisa had shared with me. Facing that Lisa loved me.

I didn't wait for dinner, but slid out to the garage, dressed in my usual hunting ensemble of slacks, silk shirt, sweater. I hoped like hell that Mae hadn't seen me, but I needed desperately to go out. There was something drastically wrong, besides Lisa being gone, and I needed to be sure that it wasn't me.

Andrea Norton was as close to a perfect fuck as I could get. We'd been friends for years. It was uncomfortable that more than a few of the women I'd slept with over the previous few months had noticed that I was hung up on Lisa but not, in retrospect, surprising. Andrea not only didn't care, she welcomed my fantasies.

Suddenly faced with a lack of interest in sex for the first time since I was thirteen, Andrea seemed the best chance I had at proving to myself that I could still perform. The good news was that I could. The bad news... It was one of the few times I came first. I'd told her I was ready at least twice. Admittedly, I usually lasted longer, and I do concede she had reason to complain in that respect. But she had not been in the least interested in why I was there, and even less in my worries about Lisa. So, I left her very pissed off. Okay, dropping the cash on her dresser didn't help.

March 23, 1985

Sid's Voice

I ran that next morning almost oblivious to Nick and Motley at my side. Mae, however, was waiting for me at the breakfast table. The look on her face told me that I was going to have to face, once again, what a God-damned pain in the ass these Wycherly women were about dealing with The Truth.

"Uh, Sid?" she asked, looking far more contrite than I'd be willing to bet she felt. "Last night, I thought about what you said about not calling our parents. I can't agree with you. They need to know."

"Alright. Call them." I reached for the fruit salad that I relied on for my breakfast.

"I did. Last night. They're flying in this afternoon."

I wanted to curse but didn't. Lisa had shared with me how badly it hurt her that the two men she cared about most were at odds with each other. I mean, seriously, what the hell do you do at that point? Nick came in, ate, then gave me a quick hug and asked permission to watch a movie on the VCR. I gave it and he ran off. Mae was still looking at me.

"Sid, something else is bothering you."

Oh. Right. As if I wanted to talk to Mae about the night before.

"Isn't there enough going on?" I asked.

"Yes. But there's something else, too."

"What difference does it make?" I said. "We're both worried about Lisa and that's as it should be."

"Don't try to evade the issue."

"I'm not evading anything. I just don't want to talk about it."

Mae sighed. "I'm willing to listen."

"I know." I started pacing. "Really, I do. It's just not something I'd feel comfortable talking to you about."

"Would you feel comfortable talking about it with Lisa?"

Damn her.

"Probably not," I said. I sat back down again.

"But you'd talk to her about it, anyway, wouldn't you?"

Damn her, she was right. I still pulled away.

"Sid, I'm not trying to replace her. But you need someone to talk to now and I'm the only one around."

I looked at the ceiling, trying to find a way out of this. "Mae, please."

"You don't have to be afraid of shocking me. I am a married woman."

As if she'd have even the least idea. "Mae, I don't want to talk about it."

"Sid…"

It was almost as if Lisa, herself, had reached into my soul. I threw my napkin onto the table.

"I have lost interest in sex," I finally said. "Completely. It's dried up. I can perform okay. I proved that last night. I just don't want to. That's never happened to me before."

"How long has this been going on?" Mae was, surprisingly to me, way more clinical than I would have thought.

I winced. "Since she was taken. Although, if I'm really being honest, probably since last fall." I closed my eyes. "Mae, what the hell is happening to me?"

She thought it over. "Sid, what's different about your relationship with Lisa?"

"No sex."

"Besides that."

"I don't know. We talk. We care about each other."

Mae smiled. "And your other girlfriends?"

"I care about them. It's not as deep, but I care."

"I'm not saying you don't." Mae's smile grew. "But why aren't things as deep with your girlfriends as they are with Lisa?"

"How the hell should I know?" I found myself pacing around the breakfast table. "You're obviously trying to get a specific answer out of me. Why don't you just tell me?"

"Don't you think it would make a lot more sense if you found it out for yourself?"

"Oh, for fucking Christ's sake!" I threw up my hands in frustration. "How the hell should I know?"

Mae sighed. "I guess you wouldn't. Except that it's patently obvious to everyone except you, and possibly her, that you two love each other. And I mean real love, way beyond having the hots for each other."

"Son of a bitch."

"What's wrong?" Mae's eyes bore into me.

"She told me last fall that she loved me." I closed my eyes and shuddered. "I didn't take it well."

Mae laughed.

"What?" I glared at her.

"Oh, for crying out loud, Sid. I did not realize you had your head as far up your ass as you do." She laughed again.

"What the fuck?" I gasped.

Lisa has a real issue with swearing, and everything I had seen from Mae had led me to believe she and her sister shared that trait.

"Sid Hackbirn, you love Lisa. That's why you don't want to have sex with anyone else. Every time you try, I'm willing to bet seriously good money, you're comparing that woman to her and it's coming up short. And I think you're finally getting that. You may call it caring and relating and whatever other terms you use. But it's real love that's the issue here."

I sighed. "Is it really that simple?"

"Yes. Not that easy, but definitely that simple." She came up and laid her hand on my arm. "Don't sell yourself short. You are capable of a great deal of love. I see it when you interact with my kids. And I really see it with Lisa."

"But I don't get it. Any other woman wouldn't mean a damn thing."

"Wouldn't she?" She looked at me knowingly and I turned away.

"I'm not hurting anybody, Mae."

"How about yourself? Aren't you cheating yourself out of a full, rich relationship with Lisa by your fooling around?"

"How?"

"If you really love Lisa, and I know you do, don't you want to give her all of yourself? And how can you if you keep giving a part of yourself to every other woman that comes along?"

I hung my head. "I want to give her my best."

"And that best is you completely. You know it, Sid. And you know those other relationships do take a part of you. A part I think you don't want to give anymore. If you didn't, we wouldn't be having this talk."

"Fuck."

Mae laughed again. "I'll let you think about this."

I didn't get much of a chance to. I went to the command center in my office. Commander Reyes was talking on the phone. My heart stopped. I hadn't heard the phone ring, which either meant that he'd made the phone call, or that someone had called on the special line that was used only for Quickline business.

"Great. I'll keep you posted," he said into the receiver, then hung up. He looked up. "I just called into the office. How are you holding up?"

"I have no idea." I frowned. "Shouldn't we have heard something by now?"

"We're only about thirty-six hours in. It shouldn't be too much longer, but a lot depends on what the kidnappers are after. Usually if a kidnapper calls right away, he's either look-ing for a quick score or has realized that his victim is too hot to handle. Terrorists will sometimes call their demands in fast because they're looking for the publicity. The really smart guys, they let the families hang for a day or two, so they're really anxious and ready to pay."

"But that gives the families time to call the cops."

"Yeah. And very few kidnappings for extortion happen here in the U.S. for that very reason. They mostly happen in places where the police are ineffective. But we had a public grab. They had to figure someone was going to call the police. So, now they're letting us twist in the wind."

I let out my breath and moved into the outer office, which was Lisa's office. Her photos on the wall, including one of me in silhouette against the sun rising in the Grand Canyon.

The doorbell rang. I went and got it, opening the door as Mae walked up behind me. Eliana Martinez, and presumably her mother, stood on the door mat.

"Mr. Hackbirn, may I come in?" she asked.

"Please." I stepped aside and pointed. "Why don't we go into the living room?"

"This is my mother," Eliana said. "She does not speak English."

Mae and I smiled and nodded at her. She nodded back. Eliana and her mother sat down on the couch while Mae and I settled into the chairs.

Eliana started crying. "I should have come yesterday. I am so sorry. But they would not let me."

"Eliana," Mae said. "We were all traumatized by what happened that night. You came as soon as you could."

"But is my fault!" she cried.

I could see Mae's frustration battling her need to be consoling.

"It's nobody's fault but the people who did it," I said quickly.

"No. You do not understand." Eliana pressed her eyes shut for a moment, then took a breath. "The men. They were coming for me."

"You don't know that," I said mechanically.

"No. Mr. Hackbirn, it had to be." Eliana got out a linen handkerchief and dabbed at her eyes. "You see, my father, he is a judge in Bogotá, where we live. The Cartel Medellín, they do not like him. My father sent me and Mama here to keep us safe from them. Only they have found out we are here."

I got up and went to the intercom. "Commander Reyes, would you please join us in the living room?"

Eliana looked frightened. "We were not supposed to tell anyone about why we came or my father."

I patted her on the shoulder. "I understand, but now we need to know what's going on."

Reyes came in with the question on his face. I told Eliana to repeat what she'd told me, and she did, weeping, but with a great deal of fortitude. Reyes looked at me, then spoke softly to her in Spanish. Mrs. Martinez also joined the conversation as Mae and I looked on.

A minute later, Eliana and her mother got up.

"Mr. Hackbirn, I am so sorry," Eliana said.

I sighed. "Eliana, you did not cause this to happen. The men who took Lisa did. The men who are trying to coerce your father into doing whatever made this happen. I saw Lisa push you behind her. I saw Jesse White pull you even further away. Lisa did what she did because that's who she is. I know it's going to be extremely hard not to feel guilty, but when you do, I hope like hell you hang on to the fact that you did not cause this. That there were two very caring people in the immediate area who were able to save you, that's what you be thankful for. That's what you hang onto. That they cared and you were worth it to them." I lifted her chin and looked into her eyes. "Do you understand?"

"I think so, Mr. Hackbirn."

"Good. Thank you for telling us. It may just help us get Lisa back safe and sound."

Mae came over. "And we'll keep praying for you, Eliana."

"I will pray for you, too."

Mae held Eliana and her mother, then walked them to the door. I looked at Reyes.

"This is an interesting twist," he said. "Might account for why we haven't gotten a ransom demand yet."

"I think I'm going to call Henry," I said, moving to where the phone sat on the wall next to the hall.

"Your FBI pal? Good idea."

I dialed Henry's office, but he wasn't in.

"Sid, I'm so sorry about Lisa," said Angelique, who was Henry's secretary. I didn't stop to wonder why she was in the office on a Saturday. "We've been on pins and needles here."

"Thanks, Ange. When is Henry going to be back?"

"I'm such an idiot! He's on his way to your place. Have you heard anything yet?"

"Not yet."

"Um, I'd offer to stay over, but I'm not doing that anymore."

I found myself chuckling. "Believe it or not, neither am I."

"Really? Since when?"

"Since they took her."

"Oh, Sid. I'm so sorry. You poor thing. Um..."

"Don't worry about it, Angelique. Listen, why don't we get together for lunch sometime? Hopefully after things settle down. We're still friends and I'd like to see that continue."

Angelique sniffed. "I would, too. Thank you, Sid."

"Thank you, Ange."

I hung up the phone, acutely aware that Mae had been watching and listening. She just smiled and patted my arm.

Henry arrived a moment later. He's a tall man with some skin condition that leaves his face in a perpetual flush. I held him at the door after making sure no one could hear us.

"The phone for the side business?" I asked him.

"Shut off for the time being," Henry replied quickly. "It's the first thing I did that night. Your courier line's also shut down." He looked up as Reyes came out of the living room. "We'll talk later. Phil, how's it going?"

Reyes looked at me and waved Henry to the office. "Come on in. I just had an interesting chat with one of the witnesses."

I went to my bedroom and locked the door. Then I punched the code and room number into the intercom. Henry couldn't tell me anything he wouldn't have told a civilian, but that didn't mean I couldn't find out.

"She was sure it was the Medellín cartel?" Henry's voice faded into the bedroom intercom from the office.

"Yeah. I asked her again in Spanish and her mother said that the cartel had definitely been threatening the family," Reyes said.

"That's good. It supports what I just got." Henry cleared his throat. "I checked out that license plate, like you asked. There's a reason it came up dead. The van is registered to the U.S. Government."

"What?"

"According to my contact, it's an account the CIA and some other agencies use for their undercover operatives." Henry's contact, my ass. He would have figured out the plate as soon as Reyes had asked him. "If Medellín is involved, then they've got help from our side."

"Why would the CIA want to help a drug cartel?" Reyes sounded pretty skeptical.

Henry hesitated. "It's mostly the paramilitary arm, which was formed to protect, among other things, U.S. oil interests."

"Yeah. I heard about all those executives getting kid-napped."

"Not to mention a host of other elite types in the Colombian government who were not friendly to the cartel. The cartel is pretty brutal, but they've done a lot to get roads paved and plumbing to outlying areas, and they're anti-Communist."

"Which makes them our friends." Reyes grunted.

"More or less." Henry paused. "I might be able to call in a favor or two, but it's going to be tricky."

"I've heard those CIA guys are a royal pain in the ass." Reyes snorted again. "Well, the kidnappers have to know by now that they got the wrong target. Fortunately, your friend has money, and if what they really need is the girl, they will probably want to try for a trade."

I felt like throwing up. If they had gotten the wrong target, it was just as likely they'd killed Lisa and run. I'm not sure what they said next, but Henry was saying that he wanted to talk to me privately and goodbye.

I slapped the intercom off and opened the door. Henry was in the hall outside the office.

"Henry," I hissed and waved him to me.

A moment later, he came into the room, and I locked the door. He took one look at me and shook his head.

"You were listening in." He folded his arms across his chest.

"Hell, yes." I tried to hold myself up.

"You know, Sid, that's why we don't talk about stuff like this with the families. Besides, Reyes is right. Lisa is still worth more to them alive than dead."

"Uh-huh."

"He knows his stuff. Hell, my office has even called him for hostage situations. He's one of the best in the business. So, you can stop panicking."

"I am not panicking!" I looked away.

"Like hell, you're not." Henry put his hand on my shoulder and gripped it hard. "Now, I need you to get your shit together. This CIA thing is a massive problem for you and me. You've got to stay out of things and keep your nose extra clean."

I shook my head. "No. I am not staying out of this."

"You're too close to the case. I'm too close to the case. And we've got to be extra sure those Company rat bastards don't find out the kidnappers got one of our operatives." He looked away, then back at me. "Look, as soon as I found out about that license plate, I talked with my Company liaison. He's not sure what the hell is going on but thought there might be some KGB activity connected to it, and the problem is, he's the one who asked me to have you two check out Danschenko."

"Fuck." I could feel the color draining from my face. "Danschenko's not onto us, is he?"

"Not as far as I know, and I don't see why he would be anything more than suspicious. Besides, you two are checking him out under your cover names, right?"

I sank onto the bed and shook my head. "We can't. Donaldson got blown last fall and we haven't been assigned new names and IDs yet." Lisa and I had alter egos as Ed and Janet Donaldson and I'd been posing as Ed Donaldson when my cover had been blown the previous fall on a case. "But I'm just interviewing Danschenko and a bunch of others for a legitimate story. What's suspicious about that? I haven't even talked to him yet."

Henry frowned. "I though Lisa said you were talking to him last Thursday."

"It was a blind." I shuddered. "I told Lisa that to get her to the party at the right time."

"Oh." Henry looked me over, then sighed. "Terrific. Just one more reason for you to keep your nose out of this and looking as much like a civilian as possible."

"What about your liaison? Does he know about Lisa?"

"I don't think he knows she's the victim." Henry looked away. "And I'm trying to make sure he doesn't find out. We can probably get the Company to cooperate if she's a civilian. Otherwise, she's just an asset."

"And expendable." I was finding it hard to breathe again, but I had to.

Henry was right. I was losing it and that wouldn't help Lisa.

"I know it's hard just sitting tight," Henry said softly. "And knowing what you can do and not being able to do it is murder. But you've got to, Sid. For Lisa."

I nodded. We left the bedroom and went back to the living room. Mae took one look at me and turned pale.

"News?" she asked, putting her hand to her mouth.

"No," said Henry. "Sid just got a little shook up. Perfectly normal and right on time."

Mae sniffed. "Yeah. I believe it."

"What time is it?" I asked.

As if in answer, Mae's kids burst through the front door without knocking or ringing. They swarmed me, then their mother. Darby found Nick within minutes and the two of them ran off to the rumpus room. Ellen glued herself to my leg, as she so often did. Janey stayed close to my other side. Neil followed.

"Any word yet?" he asked.

"No. I would have called you," Mae said.

"I thought you had the kids farmed out," I said.

Neil laughed. "I'm going to keep Mama from her grandkids? Not a good move, Sid."

"Ah. Point taken."

I did have to wonder how Lisa's parents were going to take Nick. He hadn't met them yet. Lisa and I had planned to introduce Bill and Althea to the boy the previous Christmas, when we'd all be at the O'Malleys' house, but Nick had wanted to spend the holiday with his mother. Given how rambunctious the O'Malley kids could be, I did not think that Nick's hyperactive energy would faze either Althea or Bill. But the bastard offspring of the last man on earth they'd wanted to see their daughter with? I was worried.

I decided not to go to the airport, though not to delay the inevitable.

"Someone has to be here if they call," I told Mae and Neil.

"But—" Mae started.

"He's right, honey," said Neil.

I was later told that Nick performed at his sterling best, even engaging Bill in a conversation about fishing. I must say, this did not surprise me. Nick was, and still is, an amazing human being.

But that was later. After everyone had left for the airport I was alone in the house, not counting the police in the office, and I was at loose ends. I did have to think about food and rooms. I checked the kitchen and realized I would need some extra groceries for the crowd and called in an order for delivery.

Thinking about the room situation, assuming I could get Bill and Althea to stay at the house, I realized I was running short on space. There was only one guest room and Mae was in there. What had been the other guest room had been taken over by Nick. That left Lisa's little suite of rooms. Which probably meant I had some work to do.

When it comes to what I call the mundane trivialities of life, Lisa is amazingly well-organized. It was her job when I initially hired her, and she knocked it out of the park. But as far as her personal space was concerned, she was a bit of a slob. She called it creative chaos. I begged to differ. Given how many things the two of us disagreed about, it was hardly surprising.

When it came to our bedrooms, we both seldom trespassed. That was personal space. Still, Lisa had found a way to bring an afghan or two into my room. And I had reorganized her sewing and bedroom before that day. There was something about organizing things that appealed to me, and as I tried to make sense of her closet that afternoon, I felt some of my panic ease.

But first, I stripped the sheets from her bed, found fresh ones and made that bed with perfect hotel corners on the mattress. The closet took only a few minutes, except for the shoe situation. That was a bit more difficult. Lisa loves shoes and she had quite the collection in there, all jumbled together. I got everything back in order, choking as I found her deck shoes. They had once been white but were stained in varying shades of gray from who knew what. I hated those shoes, they were so ugly. Lisa loved them and had even found a way to get some armor hidden along the sides. I got myself back under control, then went into her sewing room.

It had been less than six months since I'd reorganized it last, and it was already in chaos. I went through, section by section, getting spools of thread on the appropriate rack, patterns organized by manufacturer and number (forgetting that Lisa preferred organizing them by type of garment), fabrics and scraps in piles according to color. Balls of yarn I grouped together by the labels and then by color. The tools went on the peg board she'd had installed and usually forgot to use.

As I worked, I couldn't help thinking about the last time I'd organized her sewing room. We'd worked a case that previous fall that had taken us to Wisconsin for a couple months. I'd been sent home in late October. Lisa was still in Wisconsin when I wandered into her room feeling utterly lost.

I had tried to give up sleeping around. I'd been trying, and failing, since the previous summer. Getting the room organized that November got my brain in some order. I was still desperate for an answer to our impasse, but I did get one idea. I went to see Father John Reynolds. I lucked out and he was in his office that afternoon when I called, and he told me to come right over.

"What do I need to do to marry Lisa Wycherly?" I asked him as I sat down in front of his cluttered desk.

He grinned. "You generally start with asking her."

"Not funny." I couldn't help glaring at him. "And, yes, I did." I paused. "Sort of."

"How do you sort of ask someone to marry you?" John's face was serious, but with a twitch I would later recognize as him trying to contain his amusement.

I got up and started pacing. "We were fighting. It was about the fucking fidelity thing." I stopped and looked at John. The swear word hadn't fazed him in the least. "I just can't promise that I'll be faithful to her. So, I thought maybe if we got married..."

"I'm guessing she saw right through that one."

Defeated, I sank into the chair. "She said I'd demanded that we get married, and that I'd come to resent it and her eventually."

"And...?"

"She was right." I began pacing again. "But what the fuck are we going to do? I can't take it much more and neither can she." I shuddered. "The worst of it is, I don't mind the idea of being faithful to her. I just don't think I can. What if she's not around from some reason? John, I haven't gone without sex for more than three weeks straight since I was thirteen, and it's not like another woman would mean anything."

"Isn't that what you have hands for?"

My jaw dropped. "What? You're a priest."

"Yeah." John shrugged. "Just because I'm celibate doesn't mean I don't know how the human body works."

"But masturbation is evil or something."

"It depends on the circumstances." John chuckled, then shifted and looked me in the eye, this time fully serious. "But, let's face it, Sid. If another woman doesn't mean anything, then you are essentially masturbating with her. So, why not just use your hands?"

I frowned. There was an issue of intensity, but at the same time, damn him, he had a point. I didn't know what to say. Fortunately, John did. He invited me out to dinner, and we talked about everything but Lisa.

That March, as I placed the last tool on the pegboard, I thought about what John had said. Or tried to. The sound of children running through the house completely de-railed my train of thought.

"Uncle Sid!" Janey yelled from somewhere near the front. "We're back."

That the kids had always referred to me that way was yet another thing that bothered Bill. Every time they did around him, I could swear he winced.

Still, I left Lisa's rooms and walked up the hall to the front of the house.

"Bill. Althea. Glad to see you."

Althea, a small woman with what Lisa calls a bird-like quality to her, came right up, and gave me a warm hug.

"Oh, Sid, darling, this is so terrible," she said. "But Lisle will be alright. I really believe she will."

Lisa had been named after her German grandmother on her father's side, and so her parents often called her by the German version of her name. They're both also from Southern Florida and their accents reflect it.

"Thanks, Althea," I said.

Bill nodded. A tall, broad-shouldered man with Lisa's big cow eyes, he was a lot more reserved. We still had detente, but just barely. He nodded at me, then looked at Neil.

"Are we staying at your place?" Bill asked.

"Uh, Bill, Althea," I said. "You two have been kind enough to extend your hospitality to me. I would like to return the favor. Not to mention that if there is going to be any news, it's going to be here first."

"Well, since you put it that way, we have to accept," said Althea. She looked at her husband. "Right, Bill?"

I had to give Bill credit. He knew when not to argue with his wife, and come to think of it, his daughters.

"Nick? Darby?" I called. The two boys came running up. "Would you put Lisa's parents' luggage in her room, please?"

"Sure!" Nick yelled, and he and Darby ran off with the suitcases.

Mae looked at me.

"No word yet," I said.

It was a somber evening. I made dinner mostly to have something to do. The kids were subdued, and the bickering had increased. The five of us adults took turns refereeing. Finally, Nick and Darby went to bed in Nick's room. The other children sacked out in the rumpus room, and Neil went in with Mae. Bill still wasn't talking to me. Althea dragged him to Lisa's two rooms. I went to my bedroom, and I'll admit it, I laid in bed and cried.

March 24–25, 1985

Sid's Voice

The one good thing about having a crowd at the house was that it gave me plenty to do. I was up first, ran and showered, then started breakfast for everybody. The kids played, but you could tell they were upset from the way they kept acting up. Somehow, Mae, Neil, and Althea got them all ready for church, and by the time everyone left the house, my ears were ringing.

I started in on cleaning up the breakfast dishes, trying not to think. I'd done enough of that the night before.

The phone rang and the line for our writing business lit up.

My heart pounded as I picked it up. "Hello?"

"Mr. Hackbirn, this is Ivan Danschenko. I apologize for interrupting your Sunday, but I wished to confirm the time for our meeting tomorrow."

"Oh." I took a deep breath.

I'd forgotten that we'd set up the interview for the next day.

"I'm afraid I'm going to have to cancel, Mr. Danschenko," I said, my gut twisting. I so wanted to find out what, if anything, he knew about Lisa's kidnapping. But Henry had been right about me staying out of it. "We've had a bit of an emergency here."

"I am very sorry, Mr. Hackbirn." He paused. "Is nothing that serious, I hope?"

"Serious enough. Look. I'll call you as soon as things settle down."

"Of course. I am looking forward to our conversation."

"So, am I. Thanks."

I couldn't help wondering about that call, though. I debated calling Henry, but the family came back from Mass and along with them, Kathy and Jesse, and Frank and Esther. Kathy and Althea insisted on helping me make lunch for everyone. Frank and Esther kept the little ones more or less entertained, which helped with the bickering. John Reynolds stopped in long enough to eat and apologized because he couldn't stay longer. Bill still wasn't saying much and looked like he would explode at any second. As soon as lunch was cleared, Althea beckoned me into Lisa's sewing room.

"Sid, um, we've got to talk." She drummed her fingers on the cutting table. "It's about Bill. Ever since Janey told us where Lisa's been living, he's been a little worried. Not about the two of you doing..." She waved her hand in explanation.

"He's afraid I'll break her heart."

"I do think so. I know I was. That's why I was so glad last summer when she got engaged to George." Althea swallowed. "Now, I talked to Lisa again last Christmas, and she swears she's happy with you, and I believe her. And Bill does, too, deep down. It's just that with her being in such danger, Bill's upset and scared, like we all are. He just doesn't know how to express it except as anger."

"I understand that."

Suddenly, Bill burst into the room.

"You!" His eyes blazed and he was ready to come after me.

"And here we are," sighed Althea.

"What the hell are you doing in here?" Bill stepped toward me.

"He's talking to me." Althea advanced on him.

You must understand, Bill is a big man, and Althea is tiny. Had the circumstances been anything but what they were, I would have laughed myself silly to see that tiny little woman going hammer and tongs after that huge man.

"He's done talking." Bill reached for me, and Althea got right in the way.

"William Wycherly! You just stop that right now. Landsakes, poor Sid is grieving, too, and you starting a fight isn't going to make things easier on any of us. You need to start talking about your feelings, and your sadness, and stop being so blamed angry."

"Oh, Grandpa!" Janey came into the room and the tension began to melt. "Come on, we've got to talk."

Bill glared briefly at me, then let Janey take his hand and lead him from the room.

Exhausted, Althea found the big red velvet Victorian couch next to the far wall and sank down onto it.

"I'm sorry about him."

"It's alright." I bent and picked up a straight pin from the carpet. "I've been there, myself."

Althea sniffed as she looked around the room. "It's such a sweet little room. It's just like her. Oh, Sweet Mother Mary, have mercy on my little girl!"

"Mrs. Wycherly?" Nick suddenly appeared in the door, then hurried over to her. "It'll be alright."

Nick sat down next to her and put his arms around her as she sobbed.

"I know, honey. I guess I'm still scared for her."

"So am I."

"Then we'll just hang on and somehow together we'll be brave."

Darby came in, too. "Can I help, Grandma?"

"You sure can, sweetheart." She put her arms around both boys and held them.

I still had the pin in my hand and poked it into the cork top of the cutting table in the center of the room.

"Grandma!" called two very young voices. "Grandma!"

The twins came running in.

"Grandma," said Marty. "We got boo-boos and Mommy's crying with Daddy, and we got no one to kiss them."

"I hurt here." Mitch pointed to his knee.

Althea sniffed and released the older boys. "Well, now. We'd better take care of that right away. Come here."

The twins crawled into her lap, probably looking for attention more than anything else. Althea immediately dispensed kisses.

"You were crying." Marty touched her cheek.

"Yes, I was."

"Is Aunt Lisa coming back?" Mitch asked.

"Honey, I'm afraid I don't know. I sure hope so, and I'm praying that she will."

"Teach me to pray!" Marty demanded.

"Okay, I suppose I could. You know prayer is talking to God."

"I want to pray like the ladies in church with the necklaces that they don't wear," Mitch said.

I slid into Lisa's bedroom.

"That's the Rosary. It's a very powerful prayer, so why don't I teach you that?"

"You don't have your necklace," Mitch said.

I picked up Lisa's beads from where they hung on the brass head frame of her bed.

"That's okay, honey," Althea said. "You can still pray the Rosary without your beads."

"You don't have to," I said.

I handed her Lisa's beads.

"Why, thank you, Sid." Althea smiled up at me. "Where did you get this?"

"It's Lisa's. She keeps it on her bed." I smiled weakly. "It was an accident that I saw it there."

In truth, it was one of Lisa's nightmares that had started the previous summer. The beads were part of the glue that held her together.

I left the room. There was nothing I had to add.

Neil took his kids home shortly after dinner. Frank, Esther, Kathy, and Jesse left around then, too. Nick stayed, refusing to go with Neil with a surprising belligerence. Mae and Althea returned to the living room. Mae had asked about their relatives in Southern Florida and Althea went off on some tirade about how troublesome they were, and that her niece Maggie was coming in for trouble for not being married, and felt really bad about it, and Aunt Amanda, Maggie's mother, had tried to berate Althea because Lisa wasn't married, and I really did not want to hear any more.

Fortunately, Henry called and asked to speak to me privately. Commander Reyes had told me he wouldn't monitor obviously personal calls, so I took the call in my bedroom after locking the door.

"Well?" I asked.

"The Company liaison is acting really hinky, but I've got a feeling Lisa is still with us." Henry paused. "How good is she at jumping on an opportunity?"

"Terrific at it. In fact, I've been wondering if the reason why we haven't gotten a ransom demand is that she's escaped." I stopped, my heart pounding. "Henry, has she?"

"Uh, no. That much I'm sure of. I'm sorry, Sid, but I can't say more, and really don't even know that much more. Just that we're working on it, okay?" He paused. "It's even more ticklish than I thought, and don't ask."

"Fuck. Listen, Danschenko called this morning. He wanted to confirm our interview tomorrow, but I don't know." I repeated the conversation we'd had.

"Oh, shit." Henry sounded exhausted. "That's yet another wrinkle. Listen, you did good. Just keep watching your ass around that guy. We know that he's trying to make all kinds of friends, which probably means that he's going to screw half of them."

"Is he involved in this?"

"I have no way of knowing. I just know not to trust him. Period." Henry paused again. "I don't want to get your hopes up because things could change at any time. There are no guarantees here. But last I heard, Lisa is still alive."

I closed my eyes as my gut wrenched and my heart leapt. "Okay. Thanks for saying so."

"Just don't tell anyone over at your house, especially the cops. We can't have them getting over-excited and trying something. Just between us, right?"

"Right."

We hung up after that and I tried to start my breathing again.

Once again at loose ends, I made my way to the library. Bill was there, sitting in one of the wingback chairs and staring off into space. I went, instead to the rumpus room. Nick was there, knitting as he watched television. I swallowed. Lisa had taught him when he'd first come to us a little over a year before, yet another example of the profound effect she'd had on mine and Nick's lives. Nick had decided that he really liked knitting, although he'd told me he didn't do it up in Sunnyvale, where he lived with his mother. He didn't want to get teased by his schoolmates.

"How are you doing?" I asked him.

He shrugged. "I don't know. Everybody keeps talking about how Lisa will be okay. I'm scared, Dad. I keep trying to pray, but it doesn't help."

I sat down next to him. "Why not?"

"Well, my grandma." He meant on his mother's side. I didn't have a mother. "It was really bad. They called me out of class that day, and Mrs. Corea, the school secretary, told me that they'd taken my grandma to the hospital and that Mrs. Corea was going to bring me there. She said I should pray that Grandma would be alright, so, I did. Only Grandma died. She'd had a heart attack. Mom was really mad, at first, but then she said that Grandma had gotten the best care she could have." Rachel, Nick's mother, was an emergency room doctor, so she would have been in a position to know that. Nick winced. "Grandma always said to plan for the worst."

I sighed. Being an atheist, I didn't have much to say. Still, I had to say something.

"I don't know about praying, son. You know that. But I do know that finding some way to hold onto hope is a good thing. The truth is we don't know for sure that—" I choked, then swallowed. "That the worst has happened. And until we do, we have to focus on hoping that she's alive."

Nick nodded and I held him for several minutes more. I so wanted to give him the small ray of hope that I had, but Henry was right. It was better not to say anything.

Nick went back to knitting and watching TV, and I remembered why I'd come into the rumpus room. I got up and unlocked the cabinet where the liquor was, then pulled out one of my better bourbons, got two snifters, and one ice cube in each, and took it all to the library.

I wasn't sure what reception I'd get, but it was time to at least attempt peace. After all, the one thing that tore Lisa apart like nothing else was seeing her father and me at odds with each other. I sat down in the matching chair to the one Bill was in and put the bourbon and snifters on the lamp table between us. Bill looked at me.

I lifted the bottle. "It's a single barrel."

He shrugged. I poured for each of us. Bill took the drink, sipped, then blew out his breath.

"That's good," he muttered.

"I get being angry," I said after a minute's silence.

"Really?"

"Yeah. I remember you telling me how hard it is to watch your kid suffer. I had no clue then. I didn't know I had Nick yet." I looked at him. "But I also know how hard it is to see Lisa suffer."

"You know, I wanted a fight." Bill stared straight ahead.

"So did I."

"You could have taken me on."

I chuckled. "Possibly."

There was an extended pause.

"That is the problem with these Caulfield women." Bill sighed.

Caulfield was Althea's maiden name. Her mother, Bessie, was, well, yet another force of nature.

"Yeah, I've noticed."

We didn't finish the bottle, but we did get a snootful.

It did not make running the next morning any easier. I managed it, with Nick and Motley beside me, as usual. I went, showered, and got dressed, then went to the breakfast room to find that Mae and Althea had already made breakfast. Nick fed Motley and the cats.

Bill staggered in and Althea glared at him.

"Just how late did you two stay up?" she demanded.

Given that I was on the edge of a headache, I grunted.

"Don't make no difference, Althea," Bill said, sliding into a chair.

I got up. "I think we could both use some menudo."

"What's that?" Bill asked.

"A Mexican soup that actually does some good for a hangover." I went to the kitchen, got the cure out of the freezer, and put the container in the microwave.

Shortly after that, I checked in with Commander Reyes and his crew. There was nothing to report. I pulled Reyes aside.

"How bad a sign is this?" I asked him, figuring that would be the logical question to ask, assuming I didn't know what I did.

Reyes sighed. "I don't know. Look. You're not stupid. We both know this could go either way."

I nodded.

There wasn't much else to do. Around ten, Conchetta came in, wearing a Blue Oyster Cult t-shirt and bearing the mail, and I went through it, sitting at Lisa's desk. There were three checks, including one for Lisa, several rejections, and one acceptance. Fortunately, the due date on the acceptance was a month out. The electric and cable bills were there, too, plus one for Lisa's sole department store charge card. Bills were something Lisa took care of, but I needed something to do. I called the bank where we had the joint account for the household expenses and verified that we had enough in it to pay the electric and cable bills. I hadn't really needed to. Lisa had made sure that there was plenty in our account to pay our expenses.

The joint account was relatively new. I had told Lisa that fall that I really didn't want to consider her my employee anymore. We were, in fact, a team. Lisa, as usual, had called me on it early that December when my accountant had sent the payroll checks.

"This is why we are not fully a team," she had said, holding up the check.

The problem was that it felt really unfair to put that big a hole in her income, especially since she was still doing a lot of the chores that I'd been paying her to do. So, that January, we put together a partnership agreement and had set up the joint household account. Lisa had asked me a couple years before to help her make some investments, and we were both surprised to see how well they'd done. Which is when I'd put my foot down and insisted that she make a will. I also had her get signed in as co-owner to all my financial accounts, just in case, and she had insisted on getting me signed in as co-owner to her accounts.

So, now we were at just in case. I did not want to think about it, but I knew I had to. As Henry had said the night before, there were no guarantees, and just because he'd had reason to believe then that Lisa was alive, he could not promise that had remained the case.

Mae was Lisa's primary beneficiary. I had told Lisa that since I had more money, it didn't make sense to make me the primary. I wondered how much paperwork there would be involved in getting Lisa's accounts transferred to her sister. Since I was co-owner, I hoped that would mean I wouldn't have to do much. Lisa had made me executor, so that might make things easier.

Henry would probably handle whatever paperwork would be involved with Quickline. I would have to get a new partner. That one hurt. I got too much business. I needed a partner.

But the thought of working with someone else besides Lisa... I just couldn't imagine it.

I put the thought aside. Lisa's purse sat next to her desk. I'd brought it in from her truck, well, I wasn't sure when, but I'd done it. It bulged with photocopies, and I realized she'd gotten them earlier that awful day of her birthday. I pulled out the papers and put them on top of one of the file cabinets behind her desk. I could go through them later. It was a sizeable stack. Lisa was nothing if not thorough, one of the reasons she did most of the paper research.

Still, there were bills to be paid and Lisa had control of the joint checkbook. I finally found it in her purse. Aside from the fact that paying bills was primarily Lisa's responsibility, there was also the reality that Lisa could get fussy about how the checkbook was handled. I made sure that I put the liner between the copy paper and the next check underneath, desperately hoping that she'd have a chance to take me to task over it. I also made a point of recording each check in the register. I went ahead and paid the bill for her Broadway store charge card, too, even though it would really piss her off. Assuming she'd get the chance to be pissed off that I had.

Bill wandered into the outer office.

"Anything yet?" he asked, knowing full well I would have said so if there was.

"No." I opened the top drawer in her desk, looking for stamps.

He picked up one of the checks I'd written. "What the hell?"

"It's for paying bills," I said.

"Why the hell are you two not married?"

I sighed. "Apparently, we're not ready."

He looked at me, his big brown eyes piercing in the same way Lisa's did. "It's about you being faithful, isn't it?"

"It is. Although, it's probably less of an issue now than it was."

Bill's eyebrows rose. I looked away. He wandered off. Finished with the bills, I found myself wandering through the house yet again. There wasn't a room that Lisa hadn't touched. Even in my own bedroom, she'd left signs of her presence in the two afghans that she'd made and brought in when I'd been sick. We were partners in business. Our assets were, technically, mingled. Bill's question had been dead on. Why weren't we married? If I had to be honest, it seemed like we were, except for the sex, and that was my fault.

I kept thinking about the previous Valentine's Day when we that fight. It was the night after Valentine's, actually. Nick having been born on February fourteen meant that any more romantic celebration was put on hold until after I'd taken him back to Sunnyvale and come home. Strangely enough, I didn't mind the postponement.

It was that dress she wore. I said formal. I got out my tux, and she wore this red sequined number. It had a turtleneck and was long sleeved. It hugged every inch of her down to her hips, then flared slightly into soft drapes around her ankles. And the back was open. I know Lisa was thinking it was very modest. Maybe it was. Maybe it was just her.

I knocked on the door to her room, she opened it, and I popped a hard on faster than I had in years. She had her hair up, and her eyes glowed.

We went to dinner and the opera. Lisa's not an opera fan but had bought the tickets for me. So, no surprise, she got fidgety. That was okay. I was pretty itchy, myself, though for a different reason.

We kissed at the door to her room, and I just followed her into the sewing room.

"You are one persistent fellow," she said, laughing.

She turned away and dropped her cape on the end of her couch.

"Persistence will out," I said.

I stepped up behind her, kissed her ear and slowly did what I'd been aching all night to do. I slid my hands into her dress, sliding up across her soft flesh until my fingers were wrapped around her sweet breasts.

She gasped and leaned back into me. I whispered her name, then kissed her just below her ear and then the back of her jawbone. At the same time, I pulled one of my hands free and slid partway out of my tux jacket.

When one is on a roll, one doesn't stop. I switched hands, and still kissing her, got the rest of the way out of my jacket, untied my bow tie, then undid the back of her turtleneck and kissed the back of her neck to the top of her spine. She moaned softly and leaned into me, then slipped around and kissed me, our tongues mingling. She'd been kissing me that way since the previous summer. All I could think was that she'd gotten over her distaste for French kissing in a big way.

I moved us over to the couch and we sat, still kissing, still exploring. She undid the top button to my shirt. As we necked, I carefully, carefully pulled the front of her dress down. She slid herself out of the sleeves. And there were her breasts, sweet and round.

I let my kisses drop until my face was buried between the soft mounds, my fingers caressing the nipples. Lisa let out one of her soft little sighs and shifted beneath me.

I tasted her nipples, and tickled them, switching back and forth between the two, enjoying the feel of their velvet solidness underneath my tongue. But for the ache in my groin, I could have been satisfied with this forever. Actually, the odds were very good I was going to have to be satisfied with that. I was amazed I'd been able to push her that far.

She let out another little sigh. I tried to suck all the one breast into my mouth, then slipped back and just gazed. It didn't last too long. I had my face in her cleavage, sucking in the rich smell of her cologne.

"Oh, babe," I heard myself whisper. "These are the most beautiful breasts I have ever seen."

It didn't happen immediately, but she cooled rapidly.

"Sid," she said in a pained voice.

"Damn," I muttered as I pulled away. "Alright, we got carried away. I'm sorry." Lisa pulled her dress up. "Look, it's not like I haven't seen your breasts before."

I had caught her by accident, although she'll never believe that.

"You said they were just mammary glands."

I chuckled. "I believe I made one very important distinction."

I reached for her chest, but her hand stopped me. Her eyes were angry now and hurt.

"Most beautiful you've seen?" she asked.

I sighed. "Alright. You caught me. That's not the first time I've said that to a woman. But, Lisa, you know I don't just say things to you."

"And you honestly expect me to believe that?" She slid back into her sleeves and refastened the turtleneck.

"Yes, I expect you to believe that. Lisa, you know how I feel about you. You are everything."

"Then why is it the first time you get really juiced up, what that pops out of your mouth is a line?"

"Oh, shit." I hated it when she got me like that. "Look, I'm sorry. It won't happen again."

She got up and scrambled around the couch. "Like that's really going to stop me from wondering." She was crying and trying to hide it from me. "I feel so cheap and used."

"You don't understand. You're different."

"Oh, I'm really special," she snapped, the sarcasm pelting me. "I can see that."

"Christ, Lisa, what am I supposed to do? Swear out an affidavit? You are the only woman in my life—"

"No, I'm not, Sid," she cut in. "Not by a long shot, and we both know it. And I don't care if you say I'm different, if whatever we share is nothing like what you do with all those others. I don't know it. I have no way of knowing that what you say to me, you're not saying to some other bimbo, and I'm certainly not going to watch."

"If that's what it will take, I don't mind if you do, assuming you wouldn't be too embarrassed."

She laughed bitterly. "I could probably handle the embarrassment. What I couldn't take would be watching you make love to someone else, caressing her and loving her, and telling her how beautiful her breasts are!"

I shook my head and swallowed back the rage. "You know, Lisa, you're the first woman I've known who didn't buy into that, and the truly ironic thing is, for the first time in my life, I really meant it."

She turned away, sobbing full out. I went over to her and held her, then softly kissed her mouth.

"Goodnight, Lisa," I said.

"Goodnight, Sid."

And I picked up my jacket and tie and left her because there really wasn't anything more that could be said. She was right, damn her. No matter how different it was to be with her compared to someone else, she would never know that, and there was no way I could make her understand that because she would never sleep with anyone else. Lisa couldn't sleep around. She placed just as high a value on sex as I did. But for her, it was rare, something to be savored and treasured. She couldn't understand that for me, it was something to be indulged in, to enjoy as often as possible. And yet, she was so desperately jealous, and I had to admit, she had cause.

It seemed selfish to want me all to herself, but it hurt her so badly to think of me with someone else, giving another woman what was, in truth, hers.

I was near the living room when the phone rang. It was my personal line. I went into Lisa's office to get it.

"Hello?" I asked, my heart in my throat.

"We have your girlfriend," said the voice on the other end.

I closed my eyes. "She'd better be alive."

"Oh, she is."

"Prove it."

The man chuckled. "I will, but first, we need two million dollars cash and the girl, Eliana Martinez."

"It's going to take a couple days to pull that much cash together."

Reyes had opened the door to my office and gave me the thumbs up. He had the phone to his ear. He'd told me that I had two jobs. One was to keep them talking as long as possible so that the call could be traced. The second was to avoid making any promises. I did not want to think about what Henry had told me the night before.

"You have until Wednesday. We'll call you then."

"I want to talk to her."

"Of course."

There was a shuffling.

"Hi," she said. "I'm scared."

"Are they treating you okay?"

"Yeah. But I'm scared. I'm really scared."

"It's okay. They're all praying for you here. Be strong, honey, and... I—" The line went dead. "Love you."

I put the phone down. Mae, Nick, Althea, and Bill all crowded the doorway of the office.

"She's alive," I said. "She's still in a lot of danger, but she's alive."

The celebration was subdued, at best. Things were still very much touch and go. Worse yet, was the call I got from Henry right after dinner. I took the call alone in my bedroom.

"Sid, what the fuck did you do?" he demanded.

Sadly, he had cause to jump on me. My record for insubordination was rather well-known.

"Nothing," I said. "I actually did exactly what you told me to."

"You?"

I took a deep breath. "Henry, it's Lisa. Do you honestly believe I'm going to take a chance on losing her?"

"Shit! What the hell happened? They weren't supposed to make a ransom demand."

"Why not?"

Henry coughed. "You don't have Need to Know."

I couldn't help but think of Lisa. She seriously hated the whole Need to Know thing, with good reason many times.

"Fuck that shit. I have plenty reason to know."

"You do and you don't." Henry took a deep breath. "Sid, things are being worked out. Like I said, things have gotten more ticklish than they should have."

I closed my eyes. "She was alive this afternoon. Is she still?"

Henry paused while my heart beat out of my chest. "I have every reason to believe so."

The good news was Henry had called my bank for me and called back to let me know that the ransom money would be ready Wednesday morning. A little later, Frank and Esther came by and stayed. Kathy and Jesse came by after the Teen Bible Study. There wasn't much to say, but we did have a faint gleam of hope.

Sid's Voice

When I'd finally gotten to bed that Monday night, I slept for the first time since Lisa had been taken, which is probably why I overslept the next morning. When I looked at the time and realized that it was after eight, my stomach clenched. Neither Lisa nor the rest of her family would have called that oversleeping.

Which meant that I was still the first one up. Conchetta had left the usual fruit salad for breakfast. I went ahead and ate. Around nine, she called to let me know that she would be a little late. She was going to stop by the grocery store to pick up the groceries she'd ordered the day before.

Althea and Mae were up by the time Conchetta arrived. The three of us helped Conchetta put away the groceries.

"Sid, do not move those," Conchetta said firmly as I tried to rearrange the cans in the pantry. "I am just going to put them back."

I sighed.

Althea laughed. "Sid, you should know better than to mess with a woman's kitchen."

"But it's my kitchen," I said. "I own this house. Well, the partnership does."

Another thing Lisa had objected to when we set it up, but I'd given up paying her, she'd given up paying rent, and the whole point of the partnership was that she contributed equally to the house and its upkeep.

"Mae, please leave the chiles out," Conchetta said. She looked at me. "I'm going to make chiles rellenos tonight, and enchiladas for the children."

I smiled even though I was not entirely cheered. Granted, Conchetta's chiles rellenos were one of my favorites of her dishes. But it was also Lisa's favorite. Conchetta made them spicy enough to sear a steak. Lisa and I both loved extra spicy food.

I took the mail into Lisa's office. There wasn't much, just more rejections. Around a quarter to eleven, I heard the police radio in my office going, then saw the line for the writing business light up as Reyes or somebody made a call. I filed the rejections in Lisa's tickler file. There was a lot that still could go wrong, but even Reyes had been optimistic the day before.

A little after eleven-thirty, the phone rang. It was my personal line. I picked it up in the living room.

"We're making a change," said the voice from the day before. "Bring the money and the girl to the filling station at 115th and Normandie tonight at ten o'clock."

"The money won't be ready until tomorrow," I said.

"Get what you can and the Martinez girl. Tonight."

"I want to talk to Lisa."

The line went dead. I went to my office. Reyes was waiting for me.

"What's going on?" I asked.

"I don't know." Reyes glared at the phone. "I don't think they're playing games. I'm thinking they've lost their hostage."

Relief spread through my bones. "Lisa's escaped."

Reyes looked at me. "It's possible."

It was more than possible between what Henry had told me on the Sunday night before and what I knew of what Lisa could do, but I couldn't tell Reyes that. He looked at me as if I were going a little crazy. Reyes clearly thought Lisa was dead, although he didn't say so. But he didn't know how very good Lisa was at getting people off their guard then whacking them. He didn't know that Henry had asked me about that very possibility two nights before. It had probably taken Lisa some time to get the kidnappers thinking she was harmless, which was why she hadn't escaped sooner.

"Sid?" Mae called as she came into Lisa's office. "What's going on?"

I glanced at Reyes. I didn't want to get Mae's hopes up, but figured I'd better tell her something.

"The kidnappers are changing things up," I said. "I'd better call the bank."

"Hold off," Reyes said. "Something came up this morning and we may not need it."

He returned to the office and made another call, I didn't know to who.

Around a quarter after noon, there was more chatter from the police radio and a second later the business line lit up. I couldn't help wondering what Reyes thought was going on. Another minute later, Reyes came out of the office, pulling on a sport coat over his shoulder holster.

"We're going to keep monitoring your phones for the time being," he told me as he headed for the front of the house. "But I've gotta go. I think we've got something." He looked at me. "I'll call you as soon as I've got some news."

"Thanks."

Mae went to get her parents, and Althea immediately got out her rosary beads. I left the three of them and Nick in the living room and prowled restlessly. Henry called around one p.m., telling the cops that the call was personal. I took it in my bedroom after locking the door.

"I probably shouldn't give you a heads up," Henry said. "But Reyes already told me that you thought that Lisa had escaped."

"They lost their hostage, Henry." I blinked and shut my eyes.

"They had to. That was the only way that my liaison was going to tell me or the cops where to find the kidnappers."

I swallowed. "What do you mean?"

"Lisa had to get out of there before they could call in a tip to the cops." Henry sighed. "I don't want you to get pissed,

Sid, but apparently my liaison has known all along where they were holding her and had a crew surveilling the place. The problem was he was caught between a rock and a hard place because he has been working with the Medellín cartel and can't lose face with them, but at the same time, his bosses are pretty pissed that he helped the kidnappers out by providing the van and the safe house. He says he was tricked into it. Even odds on that one."

"Those—"

"Yeah, I know. But the good news is that he was able to figure out a way to make it work. If Lisa escaped, then he could call in the cops on the theory that she would call them for help, then let them know where she'd been held. That way, he doesn't have to take the heat from the Colombians."

"Only one more reason why we hate those bastards."

Henry sighed. "I know, but I have to cut the guy some slack, for a lot of reasons, and, no, you don't have Need to Know. I hate to keep you in the dark about the rest, but things could still get ugly. Just keep your head, will you?"

"Of course," I replied, trying to tamp down the sarcasm. "No problem. Piece of cake."

I hung up and prowled again. So, Lisa had escaped, and that gave me hope. That didn't mean that she was safe. In fact, I had to figure that she was someplace where she couldn't get to a phone, or we would have heard from her by then. I had a feeling Henry didn't know where she was, either, or he would have said something.

We got the first real news from Reyes at quarter to three. I put it on the speaker phone so that everyone could hear.

"We got an anonymous tip this morning about a potential location about fifteen miles north of Gorman," Reyes said.

"Good gravy, that's in the middle of nowhere," I said.

"Pretty much," Reyes said. "LA County Sheriff's and LAPD SWAT teams staged a joint operation. Air surveillance confirmed that the van was at the cabin, and we moved in at fourteen hundred, and we got all four of the kidnappers."

"What about Lisa?" I asked.

"That's the not so good news. She wasn't there."

"Oh no!" Althea gasped.

"It's not time to panic, Mrs. Wycherly," Reyes said. "Sheriff's air surveillance has continued running passes and hasn't seen any fresh graves and the van was empty. We can't say for certain she's alright until we recover her, but there's room for hope. It could be she was never there. We did find surveillance photos of the Martinez girl, some of which had Lisa in them. There was a room that looked like it was being used as a prison and someone had scratched something into the wall, the letters P, R, O, V, then two seven, colon, fourteen. That mean anything to you?"

I laughed. "Proverbs twenty-seven, fourteen. It's Lisa's favorite Bible verse. She was there and I'll bet she got away."

"One of the kidnappers had gotten a pretty nasty knock on the head. Wait." His voice got softer as someone else spoke to him. "No shit!" He laughed as the other voice responded. "Well, I'll be damned. You were right, Mr. Hackbirn. I don't know how she got out of those manacles, but the Sheriff's air unit just spotted her about fifteen miles to the south of the cabin. U.S. Forestry Service is sending out a medevac chopper for her now. Listen, I gotta go. I'll call you back as soon as I know where they're taking her."

"Thank God, oh, thank you, God!" Althea sobbed as I held her and pushed the button to hang up the phone.

Mae also sobbed onto her father's chest. Tears streamed from Nick's eyes as he hugged Althea from behind, and Bill's eyes were wet. My cheeks were, too.

As soon as we'd made the calls to let Neil and everyone know that Lisa was finally safe, I went to her room and got out a small suitcase from her closet.

"I'd better pack some fresh clothes for her," I told Althea. I looked at her. "We might as well pack some clothes and stuff for us, as well. We don't know what shape she's in yet. If she has to stay in the hospital for a few days, I want to be close by."

"I will definitely want to," Althea said, and set to work shifting clothes in the two suitcases she and Bill had brought.

We were ready to go when Reyes called and said that Lisa looked to be in good condition, according to the paramedics, but that they were taking her to a hospital in Valencia.

Bill drove Althea and Nick up in Lisa's truck. Mae rode with me in my BMW. We couldn't get there fast enough.

March 26-27, 1985

Lisa's Voice

They airlifted me out of the desert scrub and hills. I had no idea where I was until the paramedics told me. I wasn't even sure what day it was because I didn't know how long the kidnappers had knocked me out for.

I was cold, shaky, tired, and hungry. But at least I wasn't scared anymore. There was a team waiting when the medevac helicopter landed on the hospital roof, and they cheered as the paramedics pulled the gurney I was on off the chopper. A few minutes later, I was in the emergency room. A nurse helped me out of my clothes and into a hospital gown, then rehung the IV bag that the paramedics had attached to my arm. Getting those dirty underpants off felt like Heaven.

The nurse took my temperature, blood pressure, and pulse, and smiled.

"These look pretty good. Your family and boyfriend are here. Let me talk to the doctor, first, but do you think you're up to seeing them?"

"Oh, please." I wondered who she meant by boyfriend, then realized it had to Sid.

I laid back, trying to catch my breath in the curtained cubicle. A minute later, Sid drew back the curtain and grabbed me into his arms.

"I'm okay," I said, crying. "I'm really okay."

"I know, honey," he gasped. "I'm just so glad you are."

He kissed me and kissed me again, and I kissed him back.

"Sid Hackbirn," said my mama's voice. "You are not the only one who wants to hug her."

"Mama!"

She was there next to me, holding me and crying, then Daddy, then Mae, and finally Nick. We were all crying freely. Sid got a hold of my free hand and wasn't about to let go.

"Excuse me," said the doctor. He was a tall man wearing scrubs and a white coat. "I do need to examine the patient."

Mama, Daddy, Mae, and Nick moved away to make room for him. Sid hung on as much as he could. The doctor asked if I hurt anyplace, which I didn't. My ankle had been rubbed raw by the manacle they'd put on me, but that seemed to be the worst of my various scrapes and bruises. He pressed my tummy and seemed satisfied. He checked me for head trauma and asked me what day it was.

I swallowed. "I don't really know. They knocked me out at the beginning, and I don't know how long I was out. It's been about three, four days?"

"About five," said Sid.

"Then this must be Tuesday," I said.

"When did you last eat?" the doctor asked.

"This morning. It wasn't a lot, but they did feed me three times a day. I missed lunch today because I got out of there."

Sid squeezed my hand.

The doctor made a note on my chart, listened to my heart and chest, made another note, then clicked his pen and pocketed it.

"Well, it doesn't look like you've suffered any physical trauma. I'd advise getting some counseling to deal with the mental trauma. But other than that, you're in good shape, considering. I'm going to release you. If you have any additional symptoms, call your doctor right away. In the meantime, take it easy for a couple days and rest up."

"I will."

"Okay, then." He disappeared.

"Thank you." I looked around. "I'm surprised the cops aren't here."

"They already got the kidnappers," Sid said. "But I imagine they'll want to talk to you." He held up my overnight bag. "I brought you some fresh clothes."

"Thank you so much!"

The nurse came and shooed everyone out of the cubicle so that I could get dressed. She unhooked the IV and let me sit up long enough to get into some fresh underpants and a pair of jeans. Sid had even brought my beloved and dirty gray deck shoes.

"Oh. Where are the shoes I was wearing?" I asked the nurse.

"Your boyfriend has them. I've got the rest of the paperwork to do, but I'll try and get you some Jello."

She left and Sid came in and sat down next to me, his beautiful blue eyes gleaming.

"Your dad is taking Mae and Nick home in your truck," he said. "I hope you don't mind us using it. There wasn't going to be room in the Beemer for all of us."

"I don't mind."

"Your mother is trying to find you some food." He took a deep breath, then looked me in the eyes. "And I've got something to say to you that I should have said a long time ago. Lisa, I... Lisa, I love you."

"Sid?" I reached over and touched his cheek, my heart darned near pounding out of my chest.

"It's not a line anymore." He took my hand and softly kissed my fingers. "These past few days, I just finally had to face that what's been happening to me all along was real love."

"Oh, Sid." I sniffed, then kissed him with all my heart.

He pulled back, smiling gently at me.

"It must have been so rough for you," I said.

"It wasn't easy, and it was even rougher on you. But you're safe now, and that's what counts." He shifted. "The other interesting thing is that I have completely lost interest in sex."

"You have?"

He trembled slightly. "Yeah. Go figure. I went out Friday night just to make sure I could still perform, but I haven't been out since and haven't wanted to, really."

"Oh, my god. That's amazing."

"I don't know how long it's going to last, but I'll be surprised if I go back to sleeping around."

"Wow." Something else occurred to me. "Lost interest completely?"

He chuckled, then smiled that hot little smile he gets when he's thinking about making it with me. "Not completely."

"Good." I shifted with the pleasant warmth filling me.

"I do think we'd better wait on making promises and whatever until things have gotten back to normal and I see what I'm up against."

"Of course." I smiled. "Can I say it?"

He gazed at me, happily. "Sure."

"I love you, Sid."

"I think I like hearing it." He bent forward and kissed me again.

Mama showed up then with a bowl of chicken noodle soup and a tuna sandwich she'd gotten from the hospital cafeteria. I finished the soup just as the orderly came with the wheelchair, and the nurse gave me the final paperwork to sign.

We got home around seven-thirty. Neil had brought the kids by, and I was glad he had. The poor things had been traumatized by what had happened and they needed to see that I was okay. All of us were traumatized. Father John came by bringing with him the best wishes from the Single Adults Bible Study. My friends Kathy and Jesse, and Esther and Frank also showed. Esther brought in all the presents from my birthday party. I wasn't up to opening them, though.

Then Eliana Martinez arrived with her mother. We held each other tightly as tears streamed down our faces. Sid had told me on the way home that Eliana was probably the intended target of the kidnappers.

"I am so sorry," she said.

"You have nothing to be sorry for," I told her.

"I know. Mr. Hackbirn said so, too." She sniffed and smiled. "And I must say thank you. You saved me."

Mrs. Martinez said something, then hugged me as well.

"Mama says thank you, also." Eliana turned to Jesse. "Jesse, you saved me, too. Thank you."

She hugged him, and her mother hugged him, then the four of us hugged again.

"We are going into the Witness Protection Program," Eliana said. "My father is coming from Colombia tonight, and then we will go."

"Good luck and God bless you, Eliana," I said.

She left, then Jesse and I both started weeping and hugging again.

I did enjoy the chiles rellenos that Conchetta had left for us. Most of the rest of the family and friends tried some and piled their plates with the enchiladas, instead. Daddy, Sid, Esther, and I ate as much of the chiles as we could get.

"What a crowd," I gasped as I watched Daddy chatting with Father John in the living room.

"Yep," said Sid. "It's been Grand Central Station around here."

"Oh, no."

Sid chuckled. "It actually helped. Gave me something to do with myself."

I thought of something else but couldn't ask him about it with all the people around.

Sid invited Mae and Neil to stay over with the kids, then offered my parents his bedroom, since they'd been sleeping in mine.

"I'll just sleep on the couch in Lisa's sewing room," he told Mama. "It'll be the easiest way to deal with it."

I had a feeling I knew why Sid was going to sleep in my sewing room and it wasn't about ease. I swallowed. I'd had my nightmare every night I'd been in captivity, and it had gotten worse each time. It's one I get when I'm stressed out, and Sid has been really good about being there for me when I have it.

Finally, the house settled down. I got ready for bed in my bathroom, then peeked out the bedroom door into the sewing room. Sid was putting a sheet on the couch, wearing his robe and pajama bottoms.

"Hey," I said softly.

He looked up and squinted at me. He's very nearsighted and wears contact lenses. He'd already taken them out for the night.

"Hey," he said.

"I couldn't ask earlier. What's going on with our little side business?"

"Shut down." Sid fluffed a pillow and dropped it at the far end of the couch. "We'll probably have to wait for Henry to decide when we're back up and running." He stopped and looked at me. "Do you want to talk about what all happened to you?"

I shook my head. "Not right now. I'm hoping I'll get a decent shot at some sleep tonight."

Sid raised an eyebrow. "Fair enough."

I waited, not sure of what to do. It felt like there was more to be said, but at the same time, I couldn't figure out what.

"You okay?" Sid asked.

"Mostly. You?"

He sighed. "I think so. I suspect you and I have a lot to figure out and it's not going to happen overnight." He sighed again. "The most important thing now is that you're here and you're alright." He smiled at me. "Commander Reyes, the hostage expert who was handling your case? Earlier today, he was convinced that the kidnappers had killed you, while I was convinced that you'd escaped. And Sunday, Henry wanted to know if you would take advantage of an opportunity, which I'm guessing is exactly what you did. I am so proud of you, Lisa. That's the worst part of our side business, in a way. I can't tell anybody just how good you are. And you are very good at what you do."

"I was taught by the best," I said.

Sid came over and gave me possibly the most incredibly warm kiss I'd ever received. I kissed him back as best I could.

He pulled away, turned me around, and pushed me back into my bedroom.

"My darling, I only have so much self-control," he said.

I laughed.

"I love you, Sid."

"I love you, Lisa."

I did get through the night without a nightmare and was profoundly grateful. When the alarm on my clock radio went off at five-thirty, I slapped it off without thinking about it and slept on, not realizing that I had until I woke up for good around nine. I was reasonably certain that Sid had let me sleep in. He has no problems waking me up if he expects me to be up at a specific time.

I got dressed and slid out of my bedroom to the kitchen to find breakfast. Conchetta was there. She's our housekeeper, and she can be prickly. But that morning, she smiled at me and pulled out a box of cereal.

"I'm glad you're alright," she said.

"Thanks, Conchetta."

The day passed pleasantly, at least, until lunch. The kids quickly finished the salad that Conchetta had prepared, which left Sid, me, Mama, Daddy, Mae, and Neil still at the table.

"So, what are we going to do this afternoon?" Mama asked.

"We could go shopping," I said, then grinned at Mae. "In my neighborhood."

Mae groaned loudly.

"I don't think we can get any appointments on this short a notice," Sid said.

Mae groaned even more loudly. "Sid, we do not need appointments at any of those fancy clothing places. I don't care what Lisa can afford. I can't. Do you understand?"

"Sure," Sid said.

"It's okay, Mae," Neil said.

"No, it isn't," she shot back.

There was an uncomfortable shuffle all around the table. Mae blinked her eyes a couple times.

She sat up. "Is everyone ready to come to our place on Sunday for Ellen's birthday?"

Everyone looked at me.

"Sure," I said.

Mae glanced at Neil, who nodded.

"Alright then," Mae said. "You need to know. Yesterday, Neil got the offer for the associate professor position at USC."

We all cheered.

"So, we're putting our house on the market," Mae said.

"Y'all are moving?" Mama asked, slightly incredulous.

"Yes," said Neil. "We've got to get out of Orange County."

Mae and Neil had lived in Fullerton, which is part of Orange County, almost as long as Darby had been alive. Neil had his dental practice there, and moving a practice, no matter how much Neil wanted to teach, was no simple thing.

"What happened?" I asked.

Mae sighed. "Darby's problem last year. People have figured out that Darby was one of the kids Mr. Jefferson molested."

"Oh, no," I sighed. "He's not getting any trouble, is he?"

"No, he's fine," said Mae.

"Mae's the one who's had the most trouble," said Neil.

Mama fixed her eyes on Mae, then Neil. "I don't understand."

Neil reached over and patted Mama's hand. "It's just that we've discovered that a lot of the people we thought were friends really aren't."

"It started with our neighbors," Mae said. "Maybe a month or two after the arrest. Suddenly, they didn't want their kids playing at our house. Carol Lester wouldn't even let her kids play with mine. I started noticing that the other moms in the Marriage Encounter group didn't want to let their kids play at our house, either. Then Ruth Spinner made a snide comment about how she would never have missed the signs that her child was being molested."

"You were doing everything you could." Sid's eyes began blazing. "Even the counselor you sent him to missed it. Hell, that's why Darby was here when Nick arrived."

"It's okay, Sid." Mae laughed ruefully. "Neil and I had already decided that he should apply for the associate professor job at USC, and they asked him to come on as an adjunct back in July. But then Ruth got nasty last fall, and when I went to Janelle, because it hurt, Janelle had to say she really couldn't blame Ruth. Turns out all of them were judging me for the incident."

Sid snorted. "How could anybody do that?"

"They were blaming me because they were scared," said Mae. "If it could happen to me, as close to my kids as I am, it could happen to them. Although understanding that doesn't make it any easier to live with."

Neil patted her hand. "So, we decided that with the new job and all, it's time for a fresh start. We don't know where we're going to land yet."

"Moving pieces to re-arrange," said Sid.

"Uh-huh." Neil nodded. "But we'll go ahead and get the house ready and up for sale as soon as possible, and then start looking at parishes and schools."

"And money's going to be really tight," said Mae. "We want to get within decent reach of the dental school, and L.A.'s not a cheap place to live."

"Well, your daddy and I can help out," Mama said.

Sid shifted, and I pressed my foot onto his in warning. [I wasn't going to say anything. I wanted to, but I knew better. -SEH]

Neil shook his head. "We'll be fine, Mama."

"I'm sure you will," Daddy said. "But we can help out and we'd like to have the opportunity."

He glanced over at Sid, and Sid smiled.

The afternoon went on. Mama and Neil got into an extended discussion about what would be needed to fix the house up. I watched movies with the kids. Sid hovered as closely as he dared - he knows how much I hate being hovered over. At dinner, Mama and Daddy announced that they would be staying in Southern California through Darby's birthday on April fifteenth. That way they'd get to celebrate Ellen's birthday and Easter, too. However, they were going to stay at Mae and Neil's to help them get the house ready to be sold. After dinner and everyone who was leaving had left, Nick asked if he could go home the next day.

"I talked to Mom," he said. "She says it's okay."

Sid looked at me. I nodded.

"Sure. I'll get the tickets first thing in the morning," Sid said.

Nick gave me a long hug. "I'm so glad you're back, Lisa. I don't think I could have taken it if you hadn't."

"Nick, I will always be around, one way or another." I touched his chest. "There will probably come a day when where I am is in your heart and memories, but I will be there, because I love you."

"I love you, too, Lisa." He trembled slightly and hung on almost as if he were afraid I'd disappear right then and there.

Later, after I'd gotten ready for bed, I made a decision and opened the door to my sewing room. Sid was unfolding the blanket.

"You know, I wouldn't mind if you wanted to sleep in my bed tonight," I said. "With me."

Sid laughed. "That's quite a change."

"I can bend, too." I shrugged. "And that couch can't be that comfortable."

Sid looked at it. "It's comfortable enough, and I think we're better off keeping the status quo for now."

"Oh. This is quite a switch."

"It most certainly is." He looked up at me and smiled that sweet, really hot little smile of his. "Don't worry, Lisapet. I seriously doubt it will be that long."

"Okay. Oh, um. Today, at lunch, after Daddy offered to help out Mae and Neil, he gave you this weird look and you smiled."

"Yeah." Sid smiled. "He was reminding me that he still worries about Neil. We had quite a good little chat this morning before you got up. He's not quite ready to roll out the welcome mat for me, but as he put it, he can see which way the wind is blowing." Sid paused. "He asked me what I was going to do about you."

"He shouldn't have done that!"

Sid shook his head. "He had every right and reason to this time. It wasn't the patriarchy. He was genuinely concerned about his daughter, who he loves, and who he almost lost this past week. I told him I didn't know yet." He came over to me and touched my cheek. "Lisa, things are changing for us, there's no question about that. I just have no idea how it's going to play out. And, not to imply that I had a harder time of it. That would be ridiculous. But last week shook me to my core in a way I have never been shook before, and that includes Vietnam."

I took his hand and kissed it. "I'm so sorry, Sid. I mean, I'm not apologizing. I just feel bad that you went through hell, too."

"It was probably a good thing. It got me to acknowledge what has been going on between us since shortly after I met you. That, for the first time in my life, I was in love, and I mean the real thing." He put his forehead against mine. "I had no idea, no frame of reference for it. I just knew that you were incredibly special."

"As did I." I smiled and gazed into his gorgeous eyes. "You sure you're not going to be too grumpy."

Since one of the reasons Sid slept around was that he used sex to relax when he was stressed, he tended to get really cranky when he had to do without.

"My sweet, sweet Lisa," Sid said, chuckling and gently holding my chin. "Those five days you were gone put me through more stress than I've known in a long time, and I still didn't get grumpy or want sex. I think I'll be able to manage. Now, good night."

We kissed, and while it was sweet and tender, the passion in me grew. He groaned.

"Damn it, Lisa. I can't make the promise yet."

"What do you mean?"

"I can't promise I'll be faithful." He pulled away from me and started pacing. "Yeah, I'll give you good odds at this point. You know that I want to be. I have for a while now. It's just that I didn't think I could. Well, I now think I can. I just don't know that I can. Do you understand that?"

"I think so. I mean, this is a big change for you."

He swore, then smiled. "It's a big change for both of us." He looked at me again, then laid his hand on my shoulder. "Do you think you can hold on a little longer? I'm on my way."

I grabbed his hand and kissed it. "I love you either way. That's all that really matters."

He pulled me into his arms and just held me. I could not believe how much I loved him in that moment. We kissed and I went to my bed alone. Yes, things were changing.

W e ran the next morning. I normally hate running, but it felt so good doing something that was normal. At breakfast, Nick ate quickly, then excused himself to get packed.

Whenever Nick came to visit, either Sid or I would fly back with him to San Jose. Nick's mother, Rachel, was an emergency room doctor and worked nights. She'd only met us at the gate maybe three or four times in the entire year we'd known Nick and had gotten so mean about us interrupting her rest that it was easier for Sid or me to fly with Nick, then rent a car and drive him to his house. That morning, Sid wanted me to join him and Nick on the flight.

"I can manage here alone," I told him, although I was not entirely sure I could.

"I know," said Sid with a sigh. "I'm not sure I can manage being apart from you right now."

"I hope you're not getting clingy."

"I get how that bugs you and I don't want to be." He looked away. "On the other hand..."

I sighed, then smiled. "Okay. We've probably got a buttload of writing work to deal with, but we can catch up on it next week."

Sid grinned. "We will. Tell you what. Why don't we take a little vacation and spend some time in The City?"

"Yeah. That does sound like fun."

When we got to the San Jose airport, as we expected, Rachel was not there to meet her son. On the other hand,

Rachel's friend, Marlou Parks, was and Nick seemed happy enough to go with her. So, Sid and I let them go.

"I don't know, Sid," I grumbled as he drove us in a rental car up to San Francisco. "I think we're getting to be the lesser of two evils."

Sid sighed. "We may be. I told Nick that there was a reason why we couldn't take custody of him, but that I couldn't tell him what it was."

"Oh, great. He's only twelve. We can't dump our secret on him. That would be cruel."

"You think I don't know that?" He glanced at me, then fixed his eyes on the freeway ahead of us. "Lisa, you and I have so many things to work out right now that taking custody of Nick is actually the least of them. He's a major factor, but not the most important thing."

I sighed. "I suppose you're right."

"Look, why don't we take these next couple of days and not worry or think about our future. Let's just enjoy the moment."

I smiled. "That sounds good."

At the hotel, Sid compromised and instead of getting us a two-room suite, he got us a room with two beds. We had a lovely time, but by dinner, Friday night, I was a little twitchy. The restaurant we were at was one of the touristy ones on the Fisherman's Wharf. However, the food there was really good, and Sid had gotten us a table next to the windows overlooking the bay and the Golden Gate Bridge.

"Are you okay?" he asked.

"I don't know." I looked out the window at the twinkling lights on the other side of the water. "I'm just feeling weird. Can we go home first thing tomorrow morning? I've got stuff to do. I need to work on Kathy's wedding gown."

"That's right. She and Jesse are getting married when? April?" He looked at me. "I didn't know you were making her gown."

"I told you about that, didn't I?"

"No. I mean, there was no reason to, I suppose."

"Yeah, I guess not. Anyway, last month, Kathy's dressmaker had a heart attack and forgot to tell Kathy about it until a couple weeks ago. The dressmaker was so backed up from being in the hospital and all that she hadn't even started on Kathy's dress."

"Kathy must have flipped."

"She didn't come unglued, but she was pretty upset. So, I said I could do it."

"You've made a wedding dress before?"

"A couple of them. I made Mae's. Anyway, Kathy's dress is simple enough, and it's already cut out. I just have to put it together and..." I swallowed. "I've lost a week." I blinked. "I just want to go home and do something normal."

He smiled softly at me. "I understand, darling."

We got home around noon the next day, and I spent the afternoon happily sewing together Kathy's dress. Well, maybe not perfectly happily.

"Oh, poo-stains!" I yelped as I tried to get some gathers perfectly even yet again.

Sid knocked on the door.

"Come on in," I sighed, then snarled at the gathers. "Will you bleeping things stay in place?"

Sid stood in the doorway with a puzzled frown. "Are you okay?"

"Yeah. Fine." I double checked the gathers, then added a couple more pins.

"It sounded like you were swearing."

I had to laugh. "As close to it as I get."

"You sure? You sounded really frustrated."

"Not any worse than usual. In fact, this is going pretty smoothly." I sat back in my chair. He looked so befuddled. "Come on. You've heard me sewing before."

He thought about it. "Yeah. I suppose I have, now that I think about it. But I didn't think you were sewing. You keep saying you like doing it, and you sounded so teed off just now."

"Well, it can be frustrating, too." I shrugged.

"Oh." He smiled. "Well, I was trying to figure out dinner just now. Do you want to go out?"

I winced. "Not really. I was just going to call for a pizza."

"Huh." Sid thought for a minute. "Okay if I make chicken parmesan?"

"That sounds good, I guess."

Sid stayed in the doorway looking a little lost, then he smiled. "I'll go work on it, then."

I went back to work and got the wedding dress almost done by the time five-thirty rolled around. I still had the buttons to sew on, but I didn't want to do that until Kathy had tried it on. I looked over the other projects I had cut out, then Sid knocked on my door.

"I've got dinner ready," he said when I'd opened it.

"Good timing."

I smiled and went to the breakfast room, where we generally ate our meals. The dining room was for parties and special occasions. It was nice having Sid across the table from me, but...

I looked at him. "You know, it's kind of weird having you here on a Saturday night."

His eyebrows raised. "It's really weird being here."

"Do you want to go out by yourself?"

He winced. "Hell, no." He looked at me. "So, what do you usually do on Saturday nights?"

"Well, if I'm not going out with Frank and Esther, I sew. I read. Maybe rent a video." I sighed. "It's really nice having the place to myself." I stopped. "Not that I don't want you here. I was just thinking how nice it was eating dinner with you."

"I really enjoyed it, too."

As for what we did, I ended up getting one of my knitting projects and sitting in the library with him while he practiced piano.

The next morning, I was nervous about going to mass. I don't know why. Still, it was Palm Sunday, so I didn't want to miss and staying home didn't feel right, either. Sid volunteered to go with me.

"No. I've got to do this myself," I said. "I just do."

Sid patted my shoulder and nodded. I went and came back quickly, then I drove the two of us out to Mae and Neil's. We celebrated Ellen's birthday, which was coming up that Tuesday. She loved the set of math games that Sid gave her and proudly showed off the science apron I'd made for her. All in all, it was a lovely afternoon.

Monday, however, was not a good day. It started right after breakfast.

"You messed with the checkbook?" I hollered at him when I'd seen what he had done.

"I tried to do it exactly like you do." Sid had a habit of forgetting to record checks in the register. I'd gotten the no carbon required checks so there would at least be copies, but if he happened to forget to put the liner in place and wrote more than one check, you couldn't read the copies.

"We agreed that I'd take care of it." I glared at him.

"Cut me some slack, will you? I needed something to do."

I groaned loudly and took the checkbook back to my desk. [I, on the other hand, was laughing my ass off. I was just so thrilled that you'd gotten the chance to get pissed at me. - SEH]

It was frustrating. I was still dancing around what had happened. I had no idea why. At least, I'd been sleeping through the night without nightmares.

Henry called next to tell Sid and me that the phone line for our side business had been turned on and that I was cleared for duty. He also gave us the name of a psychologist, Dr. Robert Heilland.

"He's very good," Henry said through the speakerphone. "And he's got a clearance to hear anything you want to talk about. Listen, Sid, I think it would be good if you went, too. You were pretty shook, and I'm sure you're feeling it, too."

Sid sighed. "I guess I am. Thanks, Henry."

That surprised me, but I let it go. A few minutes later, Sid showed me the acceptances that had come in the previous week, and I went to work laying out a schedule for catching up on the old stuff from that week, as well as the new stuff coming in. I brought it all into Sid's office when I was done. I pulled a chair around to the side of his desk and laid the calendar and files out. It felt good and normal until Sid choked over one of the deadlines.

It was for the column he did for a magazine called On Our Own. The magazine was aimed at people who fooled around like Sid did. Or, rather, like Sid used to. The column involved Sid reviewing a different singles hot spot around Southern California and commenting on the swinging lifestyle, in general.

"You okay?" I asked Sid.

"Yeah. I just haven't done the research for this month's column and it's due on the fifteenth." He looked particularly pained.

I looked at our calendar. "You could go out tonight while I'm at Bible Study."

"That's not the problem." He took a deep breath. "I do not want to go out."

It suddenly hit me why. "Oh. Afraid you won't be able to resist temptation?"

"I might be, if there were any real temptation." He frowned. "I don't get it. It's not as though I have anything against that lifestyle, even now. It's just that..." He looked at me. "Saturday night was one of the most relaxing nights I've spent in a long time. Just being in the library with you. It was great and it didn't matter that there wasn't going to be any sex. Right now, the last thing I want to do is go into a smoky bar with loud music and people yelling over it to chase down some cheap tail. Especially without the cheap tail. It's just not fun anymore."

"Or maybe the cheap sex made the smoke and the loud music worth dealing with."

"Possibly." He shrugged. "Probably. Now, what do I do?"

"Try to be objective about a place?"

Sid shook his head. "I'd better call Hattie and give up the column."

Hattie was the owner of On Our Own, as well as its editor. One of the reasons she'd given Sid the column was so that we had a visible reason to know her since she was also up to her hips in intelligence work.

"Sid, I'm not going to ask you to do that," I said.

"I want to." He smiled at me. "Come on. My heart hasn't been in writing that column for a few months now. You've noticed it and so has Hattie."

"I know." I sighed. "I just feel guilty that you're giving it up. I mean, you're giving up sleeping around because of me."

Sid chuckled and reached over to stroke my hand. "I gave it up because I want to. I'm tired of that scene and, if I'm honest, I have been for a while. The only reason I stayed with it was for the sex."

"Oh." I looked at him. "How long has it been since you last did it?"

"Had sex?" Sid blinked and thought about it. "Huh. A little over a week."

"And you haven't been at all grumpy. Wow."

"No, I haven't, even with the stress." He looked bemused, then pulled me into his lap. "Who knew being in love could compensate for carnal pleasure?"

I couldn't help laughing and we kissed warmly. But then I had to scramble out of his lap because there was work to do and the phone was ringing.

It was on the business line, and I hurried into my office to answer it.

"This is Ivan Danschenko," the voice said.

"Oh, hello. This is Ms. Wycherly. How can I help you to-day?"

Sid and I had put together a business partnership that previous winter. On paper, it was clear. In real life, we were still working out where my former role as secretary ended. At that moment, answering the phone and playing gatekeeper was still my job.

"Ah. Is good to speak to you, Ms. Wycherly. And how are you today?"

"I'm fine. Let me see if Mr. Hackbirn is available."

I put him on hold and went into Sid's office. He looked up from the desk where he was going over a printout.

"Danschenko is on the line," I told him.

"Oh." Sid had an odd look on his face as he put down his fountain pen. "I should probably do that interview after all."

"I thought you already did that."

He smiled weakly. "No. I, uh, fibbed to throw you off and get you to the party at the right time. I seem to remember you telling me that you only lied about surprises."

"Yeah. I did."

"Did you call Dr. Heilland yet?"

"No. I'll get on it."

Sid reached for the phone, and I went back to my desk and found something to distract me from making the call to the psychologist. A minute later, Sid showed up in the doorway between our offices.

"Danschenko can talk tomorrow afternoon," he said. "Do you mind coming with me?"

I couldn't help glaring at him. "Getting clingy?"

"Not this time." His face took on a grim cast. "I'll explain as soon as I'm done getting the interview set, but we both need to work this one."

"Okay." I sighed as Sid went back into his office and finished the call.

By then, it was time for lunch and while Sid and I, as a rule, do not like talking about work while we're eating, I was really curious why it was going to take two of us to do the interview.

"So, what gives?" I asked as I tucked into a perfectly lovely poached salmon that Conchetta had obviously made as a treat.

Sid sighed. "It's about your kidnapping."

"Oh." My gut wrenched, but I knew I had to face it.

"Look, we don't have—"

"Yes, we do." I couldn't help snarling.

"Alright." Sid looked at little worried but took a deep breath. "The Company was up to their hips in the kidnapping. They've been working with the Medellín cartel, which is why those guys were from Colombia."

"Why is the CIA working with a drug cartel?"

"According to Henry, it was the paramilitary arm that was protecting U.S. oil interests in the country, and the cartel is anti-communist. The problem is, the KGB may be mixed up in the kidnapping, as well, and Danschenko has been trying to make friends with everyone."

"Well, we know he's walking the fence."

Walking the fence was another way of saying working as a double agent.

"True. Henry's bugged about him, though." Sid looked at me a little cautiously. "He says we shouldn't trust Danschenko, but won't say why. We do not have Need to Know."

I got Sid's caution. I really, really hated not having Need to Know.

"Hmph!"

"Are you okay?"

"Of course, I am," I said, getting a little irritated. "Why would you ask?"

He looked confused. "Because we've both been through—"

"I do not want that hanging over every one of our conversations." I threw my napkin onto the table and got up. "I've got to get back on the horse sometime. Prolonging it will only make it harder. So, just let me do my job, will you?"

"Sure."

I felt Sid's eyes on my back as I stomped off to the office. I knew I had over-reacted. It was kind of hard to miss, and part of me felt horrible that I'd been so mean. Sid was just expressing appropriate concern. Somehow, we managed to stay out of each other's way for the rest of the afternoon.

Sid called Hattie and told me right before dinner that he was going to do the one last column, but he wouldn't have to go review anyplace. I couldn't help feeling bad about him dropping the column and almost everything else that was going on.

Dinner was pretty quiet. Sid was still walking on eggshells around me, and I couldn't blame him. I went to the Teen Bible Study as soon as I'd finished eating. The nice thing about teen-agers is that they are, inherently, self-absorbed. They were still dealing with what happened, but once they saw that I was alright, their own traumas and issues came to the fore, and that's what we discussed.

I got home around ten, and buzzed Sid's intercom to let him know only to find that he was already setting up the couch in my sewing room. Part of me wanted to chew him out. Part of me knew we both needed him to be there.

"Thanks," I finally got out.

"You're welcome." He looked up. "Odds on a goodnight kiss?"

I found myself smiling. "That sounds good."

It was so warm and delicious. As we pulled away, I gazed into his eyes.

"I do love you, Sid."

"I love you, too, Lisa. Goodnight."

"Goodnight."

I'm not sure what I was doing, at first. I was just talking to somebody, then I was in a closet, and I heard the crack of a gunshot. A patch of bright red blossomed against the freshly painted dry wall.

"I didn't mean to!" I screamed. "It was an accident! He didn't give me time to aim."

It was cold-blooded murder of the worst sort, and it was my fault. Only my fault. I could have found another way. But I couldn't, and I cried because I really couldn't, and it didn't help. I was still a murderer and should be punished.

And suddenly, Sid was at my side, rubbing my back, and whispering into my ear.

"It's okay, honey. It was just a dream."

I realized that I was awake, and Sid was there. I gasped over and over again.

"It's alright," he whispered. "I'm here."

I burst into tears and leaned against him. He gathered me even closer into his arms and kissed my hair.

"It's okay. It was just a dream and I'm here," he said again.

"How did you know?" I gasped.

"You start crying."

"But you don't wake up."

Sid is an incredibly deep sleeper. "That wakes me."

"I'm sorry."

"It's okay. I've been there, too. I was wondering when they were going to start."

We'd already been through a spate of the nightmare before, right after I'd killed someone for the first time. In fact, the nightmare was about that incident.

I pulled away and looked at him. "I was so horrible to you today."

"Yeah." He sighed. "I don't know if I should be giving you a pass or raking you over the coals. But I can't help being worried. You're totally avoiding what's happened and I have never known you to do that."

"I'm not avoiding it."

"You haven't told me what happened. You haven't opened your birthday presents. You haven't even made the appointment with the shrink. And the one time I alluded to dealing with it, you bit my head off."

"I'm sorry about that. I don't know what came over me. I really don't."

"Which is why we need to be talking to Dr. Heilland. Do you want me to set up the appointment?"

I swallowed. "No. I'll do it." I blinked, then looked at him. "Just please don't let me get away without doing it."

"Even if you bite my head off?"

I started crying again. "Yeah. I'm so sorry."

"Apology accepted."

I didn't realize that we'd both fallen asleep until Sid nudged me awake just before my alarm went off.

"I'll see you at the front door," he said, after a quick kiss.

Figures, even his morning mouth was pleasant. [Yet another first from you. Trust me, nobody, but nobody, had ever complimented me on that. - SEH]

I did call Dr. Heilland right after breakfast and felt proud that I had. I set up an appointment for Sid and me at ten in the morning the following Thursday. Then there was lunch with Mr. Danschenko.

We met at a trendy place on Sunset in West Hollywood. I thought the menu was a bit on the pretentious side, but the food turned out to be quite good. Mr. Danschenko was interesting. I wasn't entirely sure what to make of him. In a way, he reminded me of Sid. Sid is, as I have often noted, not a big man. He's barely three inches taller than me and I'm average. Danschenko was even smaller. There are some small guys who have the whole Napoleon complex. Sid does not. Neither did Danschenko. The funny thing was, even if I hadn't known about his KGB connections and fence walking, I would have thought something was off about him. He seemed really friendly, and he wasn't in the least bit malicious. But I could tell he wasn't very trustworthy, either.

Sid ran the interview. He really is better at that than I am. Danschenko answered directly and was highly informative on the challenges faced by Russian businessmen in the U.S., not to mention the new party leader. I took notes, even though Sid was recording it. As we finished, Sid thanked him for the talk, then paused.

"I'd also like to thank you for your patience about us getting together," Sid said.

"Is nothing," Danschenko said. "But that reminds me. I have something for you."

He pulled out of his briefcase a flat pack of Styrofoam that had been securely taped. It was a little larger than a video cassette.

"That's very kind of you, Mr. Danschenko," I said as he put the package on the table. "But it's really unnecessary."

"Is nothing," he said again, then sighed. "With the changes in the Soviet Union, I must make as many friends as I can. I want to stay here. I've been here most of my life, since I was twenty years old. I'm forty-three. Here is better. So, I packed a little treat for the two of you. Besides, you've had a very traumatic week or so. You deserve something nice."

He winked at Sid and sauntered out of the restaurant. I smiled, but inside I was steaming. Sid didn't say anything and finished taking care of the bill. We got the car from the valet and headed back to the house in Beverly Hills.

"You seem annoyed," Sid said as he drove.

I winced. "I am. He assumed we're a couple. You know how I hate that."

"I do, indeed." Sid checked his blind spot and gunned the Beemer into the next lane.

"The thing is, we are a couple now. Don't you think?"

"Hm." He thought it over. "Yeah. I guess we are." He smiled at me. "That's, uh, going to take some getting used to."

"Yeah." I suddenly realized that it was going to take a lot of getting used to for me.

I decided not to say that, though. As I watched Sid drive, I couldn't help thinking how much I loved him. The poor thing had been through one very rough time. I didn't want my ambivalence to hurt his feelings. We'd been waiting months, if not years, for this kind of breakthrough in our relationship, and we finally had it. I just couldn't figure out for the life of me why it felt so... Weird.

When we got home, we carefully opened the Styrofoam block in Sid's office. Inside, was a round, flat jar, about four inches in diameter and about three-quarters of an inch deep with a blue lid on top. The writing on the blue label was in

Russian and in English. It had been placed between two small ice packs.

"Beluga caviar?" said Sid. He opened the jar. Inside, the tiny dark gray to black balls glistened and the smell of fresh ocean fish filled the office. "This is no little treat. This stuff is the best caviar in the world."

I couldn't help laughing. Sid was salivating worse than he did over me. [Not worse than I did over you. But close. - SEH]

"Why would he be giving us that?" I asked.

Sid sighed. "Good question."

The cats, summoned by the scent of fish, swarmed the office. Sid batted them away, swearing.

"Lisa, can you get a plate? We need to go through it. Damn it, Long John, I am not giving Beluga to a cat!"

I grabbed Blueberry and tried to shoo Fritz out of the office. I fetched the plate from the kitchen, along with a couple spoons. Conchetta took Blueberry, then, when I got back to the office, I got the other two out and shut the door. Given that both Long John and Fritz are hard-core tuna junkies, it was no small task. Sid and I focused on the jar. He spread the fish roe out in a single layer on the plate. There was nothing mixed in. I looked and felt around the bottom of the jar. Nothing. Sid did the same to the inside of the lid.

"Uh-oh. Looks like we've got a micro-dot," he said, pulling the lid's inner lining away. He looked longingly at the caviar. "We'll need some bread from the French bakery. I can call Les and see about getting some of that really good vodka."

"And who gave us the caviar?" I said firmly.

Sid's sigh went beyond profound. "It's Beluga, Lisa. The best caviar in the world. You can't get it here that easily. Cuban cigars are easier to get than this stuff." He picked up the Styrofoam. "He even packed two bone spoons."

"He's KGB, Sid, and Henry said not to trust him. I mean, it smells fabulous, but do you really want to take that chance?"

"No. It's not worth it."

I picked up the plate. "I'll spare you the pain and take care of this."

"Alright. I'll get this washed up and the micro-reader out."

I put the caviar down the garbage disposal and washed the plate. Back in the office, Sid had not only gotten the micro-dot in the reader, which looked like a slide viewer, but with much stronger magnification, but had also set up the camera stand and was taking pictures to make a copy of what was on the dot.

"It's in code in the English alphabet," Sid said. "It looks like a list of some sort."

He took a couple more shots, then turned the viewer off. "I'd better get the dot to Henry. But, first, I think I'm going to get this film developed and take a look at it."

"Okay. I've got racquetball league tonight, then Bible Study."

"Alright." Sid smiled. "I'll probably see you at the gym."

I turned to go. He caught my arm.

"I wouldn't mind a little kiss, first, though." His eyes glittered and I couldn't resist.

The kissing wasn't part of the normal I so desperately wanted, but it did feel good.

Fortunately, even though Marlene Ramsey and Karen Jones had been at my birthday party, both had left well before ten. Since Henry had made sure the news didn't get out, both were blessedly unaware of why I'd missed my game the week before. I played Marlene and lost, as usual. Karen said good night as Marlene and I crashed in the lounge overlooking the challenge courts. I saw Sid playing the club pro Lorna Mornavian in the A-level court, spraying the walls with sweat as he did.

"I was surprised to see Sid at your birthday party," Marlene said. "I didn't know you guys knew each other that well."

Sid and I didn't really spend time together at the gym, which was probably why.

"We're business partners." I fidgeted with my racket.

"Uh, okay." Marlene looked at me, puzzled.

I took a deep breath. "Okay. We're slouching our way toward the couple thing." I shrugged. "There's a lot to work out."

"You mean, like, Lorna?"

I looked at the challenge court. Sid and Lorna were standing in the doorway. Lorna looked a little surprised and Sid looked equally bemused, but not unhappy. Lorna patted his shoulder and headed over to the challenge board.

"No." I frowned. "We're in a good place that way."

"But how are you going to handle...?" Marlene blurted out.

"Same way I'll handle all his other former girlfriends, I guess." I checked my watch. "Look, I've gotta shower and get out of here."

I was still feeling a little shaky by the time I got to the Bible Study, and it got worse as everyone fussed over me. I left before the final prayer. Sid was in the library, playing something classical that I hadn't heard before.

"Hi," I said softly as he paused and frowned at the sheet music in front of him.

He looked up and smiled. "You're home early."

"Yeah. They were fussing." I shrugged, then looked at him. "Marlene asked me something interesting tonight. And then I saw you and Lorna talking after your game."

"Yeah." He got that bemused look on his face again. "I told her no thanks. I even said I had given up on sleeping around." He looked at me and grinned. "It felt good."

"Oh. Good." My stomach started doing flip flops, and I had no idea why.

"What did Marlene ask you?"

"How I was going to handle all your former girlfriends."

"Ah." Sid took a deep breath and turned around on the piano bench. "And...? Do you want me to cut off contact?"

I snorted. "I don't think you could continue to function in this city if you did that. Besides, some of them are my friends, too. I think I'll be okay. It's just that Marlene's the first person I've told that we're heading in that direction. It feels weird."

"It does."

I smiled at him. "You know. You might want to talk to Angelique about this. She's given up sleeping around, too."

"Yeah. She mentioned that. I did offer to take her to lunch. You want to come with us?"

"No. Why don't you two go ahead? I'll either hear about it from her or I won't."

He looked at me funny. "You trust me?"

"Why wouldn't I?"

"I haven't made any promises."

"You keep saying you want to. Maybe here's your chance to find out if you can."

He lifted one eyebrow. "That's not a bad idea."

April 3, 1985

G etting up that Wednesday morning was harder than hard. I'd had the nightmare not once, but twice, and after the second time, it took even longer to get back to sleep. Sid still insisted on going running that morning, and by the time we'd eaten breakfast and gone to our offices, we'd both gotten snippy with each other.

Sid got a call on the Quickline phone within minutes of eight. Then an hour later, both our pagers went off.

"I've got to pick up that film from yesterday from the Code Five," Sid told me, looking up from his pager. "Then lunch with Angelique. You want this one?"

"Sure."

I went to the Quickline phone and made the call. When the other line picked up, I gave the caller code and got the receiver back.

"Got a Code Three, Priority Two going all the way to the Red Ten stop," said the caller, a woman whose voice I recognized. She named a Mexican restaurant out in Orange County. "Why don't you get lunch at the bar?"

"Sounds good."

"Oh, I was told to tell you that Red Light is standing by. Just page him when you get the goods. He'll get you his location for the drop."

"I'll do that." I hung up and looked at Sid. "Looks like this is going to be an all-day one. I've got to get out to Orange County by lunchtime, then wherever Red Light is."

"That's the new guy on our line. Interesting."

I shrugged. "I suppose. Anyway, I'll call when I'm heading home."

"Thanks." He looked at me. "You doing okay?"

"Why do you ask?" I snapped.

Sid stepped back and I tried not to cry.

"Dang it!" I sniffed. "I did it again. I'm sorry. I shouldn't be so snippy."

He reached out and touched my face. "We're both pretty beat." He shrugged. "Maybe this means we'll be too tired to do anything but sleep tonight. Listen, I'll buzz your pager when I get home."

"Thanks." I smiled at him. "Well, if I'm going to be in my truck all day, I'm going to change clothes."

Sid winced but let it go. He believes firmly in business wear during the working day, and it's a legitimate position, which is why I usually go along with it. We work at home and that makes it easy to let things slide. However, one of the reasons my original career plan had been to become a college professor was that I could wear jeans to work. Since my work ethic is solid no matter what I happen to be wearing, Sid knew he had little room to complain when I decided that I did not want to Dress for Success, and the fact that we were now partners made it even harder.

I did wear an Oxford shirt rather than a t-shirt to go with my jeans, and a nice calico print vest. The sky was cloudless and bright blue, and the temperatures were in the low eighties already. I had my beloved dirty gray deck shoes on. They didn't have as much armor hidden in them as my running shoes, but the running shoes had been of little use recently. I still had a bit of spring steel in my hair and a couple other surprises, not least of which was the Smith and Wesson Model Thirteen standard-issue FBI revolver in my purse.

It was not a good day to be doing a lot of driving, however. Even though I tried to distract myself with multiple cassette tapes, I couldn't help thinking. Sid and I were now "a couple." In some ways, it was everything I had hoped it would be.

I loved the man desperately, was utterly committed to him. He'd offered me a lifetime commitment the previous summer. The only reason I'd refused it was because I couldn't handle him sleeping around. But he said he was done with sleeping around, and I believed him. He was far too weirded-out by it for it not to be genuine. So, now what? It seemed like both of us were dancing around that question.

I arrived in Orange County well before lunch, so I hung around at the local mall until it was late enough, then went to the restaurant in question. I got the drop in my purse as I sat in the bar. My contact and I could have said hello, but it's better when you don't. She did give me a wink after she'd gone past the chair where my monster of a purse had been hung. I continued munching on the rather lame salsa and ate enchiladas, rice, and beans. After double checking the manila envelope that she'd left, I paged Red Light to the phone at the back of the restaurant. He wanted to meet me at the lunch counter a truck stop in Ontario. He did not mean the Canadian province, but a city on the western edge of San Bernardino County, California. I told him to look for my vest.

I groaned. More driving and trying not to think. Still, there wasn't much else to do. I got to the truck stop in time to enjoy another late lunch. I had chicken-fried steak and thoroughly enjoyed it. The thing is, I eat like a horse and do not gain weight. Sid can't. I do not know why his system is so delicate, but there's a reason he's so fussy about healthy eating. His system does not handle fats and other junk food like mine does. So, I wait until he's not around to indulge. It's only fair.

I was sopping up the last of my gravy with a few French Fries, and wondering why I hadn't seen my contact yet, when a youngish man with straw-colored hair cut in a mullet and an overfull mustache plopped himself on the stool next to where I was sitting. I cringed. I knew this idiot. We'd worked a case earlier that fall and he'd totally messed up. Even Sid had conceded that the kid did have some skills when it came to disappearing when he needed to. Nonetheless, the kid was cocksure and asking for trouble.

"Big Red," he said softly. "Good to see you."

"I'm Little Red," I growled. "He's Big Red."

Big Red was Sid's code name. Mine was Little Red.

Red Light shrugged. "You two are a package deal from what I've heard."

I tried not to push his face into the counter where we sat. "You'd better not let Big Red hear you say that. He still wants to take you apart after last fall."

At least Red Light trembled. I put the manila envelope with the drop into his lap.

"This is going all the way to Red Ten," I told him.

"Gotcha."

I sincerely hoped he had. I signaled the waitress that I was done while Red Light ordered a burger and fries. I got my check, paid, and found a pay phone in a secluded corner.

"I'm in San Bernardino," I told the answering machine. "Have no idea when I'll be back home, but I'm on my way."

That was another part of the weirdness that I was dealing with. Somehow, over the previous winter, Sid and I had gotten into the habit of making sure the other knew where we were. Maybe it was the pagers. We weren't supposed to be using them for personal business, but Sid and I paged each other relentlessly with our respective whereabouts. We did check in calls to let the other know what was going on. If Sid was doing a drop or pick up, he'd call to let me know that he was on his way home. I did the same. It was almost as if we were married.

I cringed. I had always thought that Sid and I had the kind of emotional intimacy of a married couple. Only now that it seemed like we were about to be the real thing, I was backing off. Which totally did not make sense. Marriage, in a way, was what I had always wanted from him.

I put Billy Joel's An Innocent Man album in the cassette player and focused on singing along as I fought my way through the traffic on Interstate 10. The only thing that saved me was that the worst of the traffic was going the other way.

I got home in time for dinner, but not by much. After we ate, Sid asked if I wanted to go out.

I made a face. "I've been driving all over the place. I'd really rather just stay here and read."

He nodded, but with a surprisingly forlorn look on his face. I decided I could compromise, and we both landed in the library, me with my book and he with that same classical piece he'd been working on earlier the night before. When it came time for bed, I did leave my bedroom to say goodnight. Sid held me close and pressed his lips against my forehead.

"You know," he said. "I'm really liking this."

I couldn't help smiling. "I am, too. Goodnight."

"Goodnight, my sweet Lisa. I love you."

"I love you, too, Sid."

The nightmare arrived right on time. I sat up in bed, gasping, as Sid slid in through the bedroom door.

"You okay?" He sat down next to me.

"Yeah." I swallowed. "It wasn't as bad this time."

"That's good."

Metal scraped and clattered. It came from the back of the house. Motley growled from the floor.

"What the hell?" Sid whispered, getting up.

"Motley, sh. Now, come." I followed Sid to the offices, the dog at my heels. "It sounds like something's in the trash cans. Could it be a cat?"

"Not the way Motley's acting."

Sid shut the door to his office, made sure the blackout curtain was in place, then turned on the bank of monitors inside the wall unit. He squinted at a screen in the middle.

"Someone's going through our trash," he said.

"Could it be a homeless person?" I said, trying to see around his head.

We'd had a couple come into the neighborhood, but never at night.

"No. He's dressed for a break-in." Sid looked at the other monitors. "He's gone."

Then everything went black. Motley growled and barked fiercely.

"He cut the power," I said.

Sid opened his bottom desk drawer and got out our night goggles. "I want to see what he's looking for."

We left Motley in Sid's office, still barking. The intruder was in the kitchen, going through the refrigerator. Light from the neighbor's security system reflected against the kitchen garbage can in the middle of the floor. Sid motioned me back into my sewing room.

"So, are we civilians or operatives?" he whispered.

"He looks like an operative. Could be KGB checking us out."

"Good point. Civilians we are." Sid took my goggles and presumably stashed them someplace.

Just in time, too. I heard the sewing room door open and let out a loud scream. Whoever was on the other side scrambled back down the hall to the kitchen. I stumbled around my cutting table and found the flashlight I kept in the sewing desk. As I turned it on, we heard the kitchen garbage can go over. Sid and I hurried through the hall.

"Who's there?" Sid yelled. "I'm calling the cops!"

The back door hung open and in the beam of the flashlight I could see garbage all over the kitchen floor. Sid went over and shut the door. A minute later, someone banged on the front door.

"Police!" called the man outside.

I followed Sid to the front of the house. Sid opened the door a crack.

"Beverly Hills P.D., sir. Your neighbor called, said there was a prowler in your yard."

Sid glanced back at me, then opened the door all the way. "Uh, yeah. He cut the power to the house. Looks like he came in and out of the kitchen."

The officer turned to his partner and pointed to the side of the house, then got his own flashlight out.

"He probably flipped the breakers," I said. "I can get them on in a second."

"Stay here, Ma'am." The officer pulled his gun. "We'll verify that the place is clear first, then you and your husband can see if there's anything missing."

I felt Sid's warning squeeze and didn't protest. Okay, it was reasonable to assume that we were married.

I heard a cat yowl, then Long John came bolting in toward the library, followed by Blueberry.

"Fritz is out," I grumbled.

We kept the cats inside at night partly because at five months old, the kittens were still too young to be out on their own and partly because Mrs. Hemphill, the neighbor who had probably called the police, had complained to us more than once about how Fritz seemed to be eying her prize Persian. I made a mental note to contact the vet about how soon Fritz could be neutered. Motley was still raising hell inside Sid's office.

The two officers came down the other hallway, then checked the outer office quickly.

"The place is clear," the first one said. "Looks like you scared him away. Can you check and see if anything is missing?"

"Yeah," I said. "Let me get the lights on."

I went out to the side yard where the circuit breaker box was and flipped everything on. A moment later, the light went on in the kitchen, and when I went in, Sid was telling the officers that we'd been asleep when Motley began growling and barking. Someone went into our room, and I screamed, and the person left. We'd put Motley in the office before calling the police, only they'd already been called.

The cops took our information, gave us their number to call if we discovered that something was missing after all. As soon as they were gone, Sid let Motley out of the office. The dog ran straight for the kitchen and began sniffing around. I had to pull him out of the garbage can before he ate some of the chicken bones from that night's dinner. There was a trail of something disgusting on the floor with cat paw prints in it, as well.

"Oh, Sid, Fritz got out."

He yawned. "I'll get a tuna can open."

Tuna was about the only way we could get Fritz, or any of the cats to come when they were called. As soon as Sid had the can open, the other two came running in and demanded tuna. He dished it out, then went to the back door and waved the can around. A minute later, Fritz came trotting in, demanding his share.

Watching the cats suddenly gave me an idea.

"Sid, that guy. He was going through the trash and the refrigerator," I said slowly.

Sid yawned again. "People do hide things in their fridges."

"Yeah, but that's assuming he was a regular burglar. He went through the trash outside first."

"Right." Thinking, Sid rinsed out the tuna can. He grinned at me. "Lisa, what would most people do if they got a jar like we did yesterday?"

I grinned back. "They'd eat the caviar, then throw the jar out."

Sid nodded, then put the tuna can into the garbage can and placed that back under the sink where it belonged.

"Or they would put it in the fridge to save for a special occasion," Sid said.

"Or they might eat the caviar and save the jar as a souvenir."

"What they wouldn't do is check for a microdot."

"Where's the jar?" I asked. Motley finished lapping up whatever the cats had tracked through on the floor and whined.

"I gave it to Henry." Sid gazed unseeing toward the office. "Could it be possible that Danschenko gave us that jar on purpose, figuring we were civilians, then sent someone to retrieve it?"

"That makes sense. But why do something like that?"

Sid shrugged. "If he's being watched by somebody and needed to get that microdot to someone else, that would be a convoluted way to do it, but probably safer than keeping it on him."

"Or maybe he's setting somebody up." I bit my thumbnail.

"That's probably more than likely." Sid yawned again and stretched. "Just who is he trying to set up?"

"That's a good question. Should we call Henry?"

"Sure. I'll have to try and crack that code tomorrow, too. Or... This morning, actually. What time is it?"

I looked at the read out on the microwave oven. "Three-thirty-seven."

"Oh, crap. So, what do we have on the docket?"

I yawned. "Dr. Heilland at ten, then writing work, then I'm serving at Holy Thursday mass at seven."

"Tell you what, honey. Do you mind coming to bed in my room? The bed's bigger and we'll get more sleep."

My heart did flip flops and I swallowed as the warmth filled me. Sid, however, saw something different.

"Your virtue will be safe." He put his arm around my shoulders, and we staggered toward his room. "I'm too tired to do anything."

"Okay." I said, feeling a little disappointed, but also kind of excited.

I had been in Sid's bedroom before. If he got sick or something, or if Conchetta hadn't emptied his laundry hamper when I needed some extra clothes to wash with some fabric I'd bought. I had never, however, been in his bed, even without him in it. Sid's room was tastefully decorated in dark colors, with rosewood modern furniture, and the bed was a king-size waterbed.

The waterbed, by the way, was not about his sex life. [Though it didn't hurt. - SEH] Sid had gotten hooked when he'd stayed at someone else's place, and she'd had a waterbed. He said it was the most comfortable bed he'd ever slept in.

Sid pulled up the covers and helped me in, then went around to the other side. The bed rocked as he climbed in.

"Oh, wow," I gasped.

"Goodnight, honey." The bed rocked again as Sid rolled over and gave me a warm kiss. "I love you."

"I love you. Goodnight."

I wanted to keep kissing, but Sid rolled away and was soon chattering in his sleep as he always did.

April 4-7, 1985

I awoke the next morning to the sound of Sid cursing.

"Wha...?" I moaned.

"We overslept." The bed rocked as Sid rolled onto his back. "It's after eight-thirty."

I struggled upright. "We've got to leave here by nine-thirty to get to the appointment."

"I guess we're not running this morning." Sid rolled onto his side.

I tried to get out of the bed through the rocking and flopped back, panting.

"How am I going to sleep on this thing?" I groaned.

Sid burst into laughter.

"It's not funny!" I swatted at him. "I've gotta get in the shower and we need breakfast. Now, how the heck do I get out of this thing?"

"Roll your legs over to the side and off, then use the side to push yourself up."

It worked. I rushed to my bathroom, on the other side of the house, got showered and was in a nice plaid skirt, blue blouse, and dark blue wool jacket before Sid got to the breakfast room.

Sid drove to the psychologist's office. He was in one of his more annoying moods, the one where he finds what I'm doing or how I'm reacting vastly amusing but will not share the joke. [You had just asked how you were going to sleep in my bed. As in, on a permanent basis. Yes, I was happy. - SEH] So, maybe I was not in the best frame of mind when we got to Dr. Heilland's office. There was the usual paperwork. Sid and I each filled out our forms. When the receptionist finally ushered us into the office, I almost balked.

Dr. Heilland was on the tall side of average. He wore a blue chambray shirt over khaki slacks, and his hair, what there was of it, was light gray. His lower face was covered with a light gray beard, neatly trimmed. Avuncular was the word that sprang to mind, as in his whole demeanor was of that comforting uncle who always liked you.

"Good to meet you," he said, still standing. He indicated the couch near his desk. "Why don't you two have a seat?"

Sid and I sat down.

"So, I understand we've got a trauma issue to deal with," Heilland sat down in another chair, and opened his notebook.

"Yeah," said Sid. He went on to describe the incident and how I'd been recovered.

"How long have you two been working together?" Heilland asked.

"About two and a half years," I said.

"And how long have you been married?"

"What?" I yelped.

"We're not married," said Sid softly.

"Oh." Heilland blushed. "I am so sorry. From the way Mr. James was talking... I'm so sorry. I must have misunderstood." He looked at us then gathered himself together. "So, you do seem remarkably close to each other. Can you tell me what, exactly, your status is?"

"Unknown," said Sid. "We're trying to figure things out."

"It's a long story," I said, trying to blink back tears.

Sid, bless him, went on to describe his former lifestyle and my difficulties with it. The strange thing was, while Dr. Heilland got the religion part of my outlook, he didn't seem to be buying my objections on that basis.

"You don't seem that comfortable with getting married," he said, finally.

"No. It's what I want," I insisted. "I want to be with Sid. I love him."

"I believe that," Heilland said.

The other weird thing was that we didn't really get to talking about my trauma. Just Sid's and my relationship.

"You okay?" Sid asked as he drove us home.

I thought for a moment. "I don't know. It used to be that everyone assumed that we were sleeping together and that peeved me because we weren't, and they were judging me for doing it. And I have to say that hurt. Now, everyone seems to assume we're married, which I sort of get. It's not like we aren't close. I don't know. It's something about the assumption that gets to me. Like we can't define who we are. Everyone else gets to."

Sid shook his head. "People will always make assumptions. We can't do anything about that."

"Says my favorite control freak."

"You're right." Sid glanced at me before changing lanes. "But we have always said that we get to define the terms of our relationship. This is yet another time when we do. Frankly, I do not give a damn what other people decide about us." [Damn was not the term I used. – SEH]

I sighed. "Easy for you to say."

"Possibly. Probably. Nonetheless, we are up against societal norms. Those are always hard to negotiate. But the bottom line is how we choose to work within those norms, not how others want to classify us."

I closed my eyes. "You're right." I took a deep breath. "I do want to be with you, Sid. That's the most important thing to me. I hope you understand that."

He chuckled. "I think I've got that part."

There was yet another nightmare that night. We were still in my bedroom for some reason. [I couldn't make the promise yet. - SEH] Sid held me, and I fell asleep, but woke up alone.

Henry called that morning to let us know he'd sent the microdot upline.

"It's a Company code," he told us over the speaker phone.

"Coming from a KGB operative," Sid said.

"Yeah, and not just any KGB operative. Don't worry about it, though. We'll take care of it."

Sid looked at me as we hung up.

"You're going to try to break it," I said.

He nodded. "Absolutely."

"We do have writing work to do."

"In between times," he replied.

I took off in the middle of the afternoon to go to the Good Friday services at my church. The next day, Saturday, I spent most of in my sewing room working on several different projects. I tend to cut out several sewing projects at one time, then work on them together. More time elapses between when I start a project and finish it, but overall, I spend less time per project doing the actual sewing. Oh, and Kathy came over and we did a fitting on her wedding dress. I was decidedly pleased that I didn't have to do any additional alterations. After I got the buttons in the right place, all I would have to do was get the hem in and Kathy hadn't brought the right shoes, so that was going to have to wait, and we still had two weeks until the big day.

The problem was the party that Sid and I were going to that night. Sid could tell that I was less than enthusiastic.

"We don't have to go," he told me as I picked up the small gaily wrapped box after dinner.

"Yes. We do," I said. "It's for Kathy and Jesse and we have to go."

Given that I was one of Kathy's bridesmaids and that she was one of my closest friends, Sid couldn't really argue. I had on a nice dress and heels. Sid wore a nice two-piece suit over a pink silk broadcloth shirt and colorful tie.

"So, it's wedding related," Sid said. He helped me into the seat of his Beemer. "That really has nothing to do with us."

"Yeah. Right." I glared at him. "They've got us pegged as a couple."

"Okay." Sid did sound a little hesitant as he slid behind the wheel. "But I thought you said Frank and Esther were going and they're not a couple, per se."

"Only in their own minds, Sid. We both know that." I pulled the Thomas Guide map book out from under the front seat and looked up the address for where the party was.

"But does the rest of your group?" Sid backed down the driveway.

I shrugged. "It's still a wedding shower. I hate showers."

"How bad could it be?"

"How enthralling does kitchen bingo sound?"

"Point taken. But that doesn't mean we have to go."

"Yes, we do. And we need to get over to La Cienega and head south."

"Why do we need to go?" Sid gunned the Beemer as he turned left onto Sunset through a tiny gap in the traffic.

"Because Jesse, in what I have to assume was an act of desperation, asked you to come with me, and you said yes."

It had, in fact, happened before my ill-fated birthday party.

"Fair enough. But I still think you're overreacting."

"Hmm!" I snorted, but he would find out soon enough.

You see, the wedding culture among my friends at church was... Well, kind of scary. Admittedly, most of the people in the Single Adults Bible Study were at that age when people tend to get married, so there had been a fair number of weddings over the previous couple of years. Particularly bad were Janet Weinstock, née MacDonald, and Sylvia Perez, née Podrano, both of whom seemed to think that getting married was the most exciting thing in the world and every bride wanted showers and parties and lots of presents, never mind that some of us had everything we wanted or needed and did not. The only reason we were at a couples' shower as opposed to the more traditional one was that Kathy's sister, Estelle, had made a big deal about doing it. I also happened to know that Estelle's big deal had more to do with Kathy asking her to make a big deal of it rather than let Janet and Sylvia decide that Kathy had to have a shower. It was a stroke of genius on Kathy's part.

Sadly, Janet and Eric had already arrived when we got to Estelle's house in Baldwin Hills, as had Sylvia and Manuel. Estelle had the same dark chocolate skin that Kathy had, but Estelle was a little shorter than Kathy and wore her black hair down and straightened. Leon, her husband, wore dreads. Estelle was an attorney in the juvenile courts and Leon directed commercials and the occasional TV episode. He's why Estelle can afford to work where she does. Leon welcomed us into the house and took the gift. Jesse met us in the hallway. I gave him a big hug, then he shook Sid's hand.

"Sid, I want to apologize now," Jesse said.

I groaned. "They're in full wedding mode, aren't they?"

Jesse nodded dismally. "Worse yet, they've decided you two are next."

Sid held his hands up. "They can make all the assumptions they want. It has nothing to do with us."

Jesse and I looked at each other and went into the living room, where we greeted Erin and Carl MacArthur. Maryann and Michael Dreyer ignored me, but I was fine with that. They can be very judgmental, and they really don't like Sid or that I live in his house. I was also surprised to see Lety and Reuben Sandoval there. Lety oversees the Eucharistic Ministers (which Jesse and I both are), but Reuben doesn't go to church and seldom shows up at church-related parties.

The living room opened into the dining room, where a dessert buffet had been set up. I left Sid as he chatted with Esther and Frank and got myself a plate of treats. I was happy to see that the party wasn't dry, probably another reason Kathy had prevailed upon her sister to host it. If Sarah and Dan Williams had, it would have been. Sarah said hi to me as I got a glass of wine. Dan just nodded.

"Lisa!" Janet crowed. She's medium-height and model-thin.

She and Sylvia scurried up and gave me big hugs in spite of the fact that my hands were full with a plate and a wine glass.

The two look remarkably alike, including their bottle-blonde hair, although Sylvia's roots are generally darker. Irene and Esteban Sanchez both rolled their eyes at me in sympathy.

"Aren't you so excited?" Sylvia's eyes shone.

"About Kathy and Jesse? Sure," I said.

"What about you and Sid?" Janet nudged me.

"I'm sorry." I smiled. "I'd really rather not talk about that right now. I want to stay focused on Kathy and Jesse. It's their night."

"Of course," said Sylvia.

"I'll just say this," Janet said, her voice carrying throughout the room. "We are going to have so much fun when you two get married."

My smile grew tight. "You're assuming we're getting married. We may just decide to shack up, you know."

Sylvia and Janet laughed nervously, shooting glances behind me. I had a bad feeling I knew who was there.

"Lisa, you are just too funny," Sylvia said, and the two moved off.

I turned. "Hi, sweetie."

Sid was chuckling. "Did I just hear you suggest that we shack up?"

"They already think we are," I grumbled.

"Hey." He touched my arm. "It doesn't matter. We know the truth."

I sighed, then smiled at him.

"Some shower," Esther suddenly shouted. "When do we get to take our clothes off?"

"I will if you will," Sid shouted back.

"Will you two not get started?" Sarah Williams groaned in the awkward silence that had followed.

Sid and Esther shook their heads and sighed. I love Esther Nguyen, but the only person I know who has a dirtier mind than hers is Sid. When the two of them get together the air can get pretty blue with the innuendos and double talk. The worst of it is, Sid has no problem being naked no matter who is around, and Esther will rise to a challenge like a trout to the fly. I did not want to think about that possibility.

The rest of the party wasn't as bad as it could have been. We only played one game, a version of The Newlywed Game. First, the guys got sequestered, while we women wrote down what we thought they'd answer to some rather stupid questions. Then we came back together and compared answers, each couple getting a point when their answers agreed. Then the women got sequestered.

"You doing okay?" Kathy asked me.

"Yeah." I looked around the large backyard. The other women had broken down into small groups. I kept my voice low. "Sid and I are figuring things out. He's decided he doesn't want to sleep around anymore. He just wants to be sure it's permanent before making any commitments."

"That's great," Kathy said. "I'm so happy for you, Lisa."

I shrugged. "It's just really awkward right now, and, let's face it, Janet and Sylvia did not help tonight."

Kathy groaned. "I cannot believe how dense those two are. Tim and Donna aren't here because of them." She sighed. "They may be breaking up, anyway."

Tim and Donna had been a couple since I'd known them.

"Oh, no."

"Tim doesn't want to make a commitment and Donna is getting fed up." Kathy shrugged. "I can't blame her, either. He's been stringing her along for six years."

"That long? I didn't know that."

"I'm afraid so."

I put my hand on her arm. "How are you doing?"

"Okay. I'm a little nervous. It's a big step. But it's one I've been waiting for a hell of long time, so I'm good. I'm looking forward to it, and it doesn't hurt that I'm already at his place."

It wasn't public knowledge, but Kathy had already moved over to Jesse's condo in February. The lease on her place had expired and it hadn't made sense for her to get a new place.

"I'm glad," I said. "I really am."

The women got called in and the game went on. It was a lot more fun than I'd thought it would be. Janet and Eric got into a small tiff over why had he sold his Mustang if that was the car he'd want to own if he could have any car he wanted. Then Dan Williams confessed that I was the last girl he'd dated before meeting Sarah, which caused quite a ripple of laughter.

I'd been a little stuck on that question. I'm not sure why I said Andrea Norton's name. I just remembered that Sid had said something about going out to be sure he could perform, and that Andrea was somebody he could call on at any time, and, come to think of it, did when he was bugged. I was shocked when Sid said that Andrea Norton had been his last, um, probably not a date, but close enough.

I wasn't the only one shocked. Michael Dreyer pursed up his lips.

"What's the matter, Mike?" Leon asked.

"I was just remembering where I'd seen that name last," Michael said.

Sid laughed. "If you know her, I wouldn't say anything."

"I read it in the newspaper." Michael sniffed. "She was arrested, I'm afraid." He wasn't afraid.

"How did I miss that?" Sid asked, jovially. "Too bad for her."

"What was she—" Esther started.

"Never mind," I said, suddenly worried that I knew what for. "Who's next?"

As it turned out, most of the couples, including the Weinstocks and the Dreyers, bombed out completely. Estelle and Leon got only three points. Sid and I, Esther and Frank, and Kathy and Jesse had each missed one question. The one Sid and I had missed was what was my pet name for him. I'd said I didn't have one, but he'd written down that I called him a reprobate often enough. I did, but I didn't really consider it a pet name. It was more of a joke, and as I thought about it, about as accurate as when he teased me about being an ice maiden. Sid frequently pointed out that the joke was that he knew I was anything but. I swallowed and caught my breath and hoped that no one had noticed.

Thank God, the cake was served right before Kathy and Jesse opened their gifts. Kathy made a point of getting a pair of scissors and cut the ribbons off the packages.

"Don't you want to know how many kids you're going to have?" Janet giggled.

Sid looked at me funny. I waved that I'd explain later.

Most of the gifts were the usual household items one got at a wedding shower. Kathy was very gracious, more than I would have been, even though she and Jesse had been having enough trouble trying to integrate two households' worth of kitchen equipment, sheets, furniture, and other stuff into one. She did scream when she saw Sid's and my gift.

"Court-side seats! Oooo-eeee!" She pumped her legs up and down and Jesse laughed like a hyena.

"And dinner, too!" Jesse crowed. "Thanks, you guys."

Calling Kathy and Jesse Lakers fans would have been understating it, and we'd gotten them tickets.

With the presents unwrapped, and a couple more bottles of wine open, the party was mellowing out nicely. Sarah managed to stop Frank from spiking the punch. We were mostly spread around the living room when Janet did the worst.

"So, Sid and Lisa, when are you going to announce?" she asked loudly.

"You're assuming we will," I said with an icy smile.

"Oh, come on," said Sylvia.

Sid cleared his throat. "If and when we decide to announce, we will do it when we're damn good and ready and not before."

"Anybody want more cake?" Estelle asked, and there were quite a few takers.

On the way home, Sid was... I don't know how to describe how Sid was, but he wasn't entirely happy.

"So, what was the thing with the ribbons?" he asked.

I rolled my eyes. "It's an old gag that the number of ribbons you break unwrapping your gifts at the wedding shower is the number of children you'll have. Janet and Sylvia think it's hysterical and probably nicked most of the ribbons to make them break more easily. At least, they did at Sarah Williams' shower."

"Why do you put up with those two?" Sid checked his blind spot, then gunned the car into the next lane and around two other cars.

I sighed. "When they're not in wedding mode, they're actually pretty nice women. There's just something about showers and weddings that flips a switch in their brains, and they become impossible."

He glanced at me. "Shacking up?"

"You have no idea how attractive that sounds right now."

"You know, we probably could, and they wouldn't be any the wiser."

I stirred, feeling the warmth rising. "Except that they already think we are."

Sid grunted. "So what? As for the wedding thing, how bad an assumption is it?"

"I don't know. Not bad, I guess." I glared out the side window. "It's not the odds that's the issue. It's that they assume it's going to happen. Don't I get to be the one who decides that I'm getting married?"

He chuckled. "I hope I get some say in that."

"You're the only one who does." I looked over at him, then looked away. "Sid, do you want to get married?"

He blew his breath out. "You know my training on that one. Still, I can't really call it a crock anymore. And if I'm honest, the whole lifetime commitment thing, even with fidelity, that doesn't bother me." He glanced at me, then turned his attention back to the road ahead. "I know what promise I want to make to you. What happens after that, whether we just share a bedroom or get Father John to wave his hands over us doesn't really make much difference to me. Which is why I don't mind going along with whatever makes you feel comfortable."

"Comfortable. Interesting way to put it."

He looked at me, then again, focused on the road.

I had three nightmares that night. Sid and I were both dragging the next morning, but I made it to Easter mass on time then visited my shut-ins. By the time I got back, Mae, Neil, the kids, and Mama and Daddy had all arrived at the house. It was a happy, chaotic day, with no questions about my future, about Sid, about anything. That night, I slept through until morning undisturbed by any dream at all.

April 8–9, 1985

I'll admit it. I do not use swear words. I was thinking about it some months ago and I realized it was how I was raised. When I was growing up, there were few things that would get mine or Mae's fannies tanned faster than using a bad word. Even darn or stupid were pushing it. Mama was not oppressive about it. You just did not do it and that was that.

I don't get weird about other people using foul language. Sid, for example, has quite the foul mouth and I don't usually object, except when he uses Jesus' name in vain. That one does bug me.

So, when I state that what happened that afternoon, the Monday after Easter, made me come about as close to swearing as I have in a long time, you can bet I was at my limit.

It started mildly enough. Ivan Danschenko called to see if Sid had any additional questions. I put him on hold.

"That's interesting." Sid sorted through his notes, then looked up at me. "You know, I do have a question or two. Do we want to assume he thinks we're civilians?"

"Probably not a bad idea."

Sid nodded and picked up the phone. "Mr. Danschenko, how are you today?"

I went back to my office and looked over some interview notes for another article we were working on.

"Lisa," Sid called. "Are you okay with another lunch meeting with Danschenko today?"

"Sure." I wasn't okay with it, but we were still investigating Danschenko.

A minute later, Sid leaned on the door jamb between the offices. "He wants to meet us at his warehouse."

"Is he setting us up?" I bit my lip.

"We'll find out, I guess. Will you be ready to leave in an hour?"

I looked over my notes. "I should." I sighed. "I'm missing something. There should be one more deadline coming up, but I can't find it." I looked up and glared at him. "You didn't re-organize my tickler file, did you?"

"No. I just put some rejection letters in there."

I sighed and went back to looking through the papers in my inbox and the tickler file. I hated it when we got behind. Inevitably, something would be missed, and we wouldn't find it until right on top of when it was due. Fortunately, we had yet to miss a deadline and I wasn't about to let it happen.

I tried to put all that out of my mind as Sid drove us to the warehouse near the airport. Neither of us said much. With no idea of what we were getting into with Danschenko, both Sid's and my nerves were on high alert. We were both armed to the teeth, even though it didn't show. The problem was that if we wanted to keep our covers intact as civilians, we wouldn't exactly be able to draw any weapons.

We parked near the door to the warehouse office. It was in an industrial park filled with cement block buildings all painted white. The office door was glass, and next to it, there was a huge roll-up door, which was closed. Besides the suite number and some gold lettering on the glass office door, there were few clues as to what was inside.

Danschenko was in the foyer, sitting behind the receptionist's desk.

"Good to see you, Mr. Hackbirn, Ms. Wycherly." He stood and shook our hands. "Come. I will give you a little tour of my business."

Behind the receiving area, there was another larger office, where most of the paperwork was done. There were two doors at the back, one leading to another office with a one-way window facing out so that we couldn't see inside, the other door leading to Danschenko's office. Near the door to the warehouse there was a huge refrigerator, which housed all the caviar the business imported. I could see Sid salivating as we walked past.

"Did you enjoy your little treat?" Danschenko asked.

"That was some little treat," said Sid. "We enjoyed it very much. Thank you."

The warehouse was empty of people. The employees had all gone for lunch, apparently.

"I do not need that many, so this is what happens."

Pallets of crates and cardboard boxes were scattered about the floor near the front roll-up. A ladder in the far corner led to the roof, and under it was a back door. Freestanding shelves of all kinds stood in rows next to the back wall. Over at the far side of the front was a packing and mailing station. Danschenko showed us his inventory system, then took us back into the main office.

"My office is here." He showed us to the small room at the back. Papers and boxes were everywhere and on the back credenza stood a brass samovar.

"Now, shall we go to lunch?" he asked.

We followed him to the front office door, but as he put his hand out to open it, gunfire echoed against the cement buildings and bullets shattered the glass just in front of Sid and me. I didn't have to pretend to be afraid. I was. I screamed.

"What the hell?" Sid yelled.

Danschenko pushed us back into the main office, and slammed the door shut. He pulled an automatic out of a shoulder holster. I screamed again. He sighed and pointed to the room with the one-way window.

"Hurry. Hide there. Is me they want." He looked out the door to the front of the building.

"What the hell are you trying to pull?" Sid hollered as he pushed me toward the side room.

"Never mind." Danschenko looked back at us apologetically. "You'll be safe in that other office. They can't see you." He nodded and waved us to the room. "They're coming. I'll go out the back. I see two. You wait until they come through, then go out the front. Stay low just in case."

I moaned as Sid shut the office door. We bent just enough to see out of the one-way glass without exposing ourselves in case a stray bullet or two came our way.

Danschenko stayed in the front office long enough for two men in faded jeans and black shirts to burst through the outside door. They both carried automatic rifles. I gasped as I slid my hand into my purse and got a grip on my Model Thirteen. Sid had his left hand behind his back, where good odds he had at least a twenty-two in a back holster. The two men saw the door to the warehouse closing and ran after. I looked at Sid as the door closed behind them.

He nodded and pulled his hand out empty. "Let's go."

I kept my hand in my purse. Sid got through the front door first, staying low and watching everywhere. He usually goes to the front, and I take the rear because I'm the better shot. We scurried over to the car, but no one was about. Sid poked his head up cautiously.

"Looks like we're clear," he said breathing heavily.

I got up then yelped when I saw the hole in his jacket at the shoulder. White stuffing and interfacing stuck out through the back side.

"Sid, you're hurt!"

"I'm fine," he said, then looked down at his shoulder. "Damn it, I liked this suit."

I pushed the jacket away and looked underneath. His snowy white shirt and dark vest were unmarked. I closed my eyes in relief.

"Looks like it just went through the shoulder pad," I gasped.

"Let's get out of here." Sid whipped the jacket the rest of the way off and tossed it into the back seat while I ran around to the passenger side.

A minute later, the Beemer roared out of the industrial park.

"Well, that answers one of our questions," Sid said as he dodged cars and headed up Sepulveda Avenue.

I tried to control how badly I was shaking. "He thought we were civilians."

"He's either a hell of an actor or he bought it."

"I'll go with he bought it." I suddenly started crying. "Sid, those two men, though. I recognized them."

"What?"

"They were two of the kidnappers."

Sid swore. "You're sure?"

"Yes!" I shut my eyes and dug into my purse for a tissue. "But why would they be after Danschenko?"

"KGB was involved somehow." Sid cursed. "That must have been Danschenko."

"I thought the cartel was anti-communist. That's why the Company is working with them, isn't it?"

"Sort of. We need to talk to Henry." He looked over at me. "You look a little rattled."

I took a deep breath. "I am, but I'll be okay." I blinked and suddenly smiled. "In some ways, it actually feels a little on the normal side, at least, normal for us."

Sid couldn't help chuckling. "It does, doesn't it?"

"Can we go to lunch?" I finished wiping my eyes. "I'm starving."

"That is a constant with you, but let's."

"Then we have to get back. We're getting more and more behind by the minute."

Sid made a point of calling Henry James about what had happened with Danschenko. Henry, apparently, didn't have much to say, which did not make Sid any too happy. I left it at that. I was pretty sure there was something we really Needed to Know, but that didn't mean we were going to find out. That evening I went to the Teen Bible Study. When I got back Sid was waiting for me on the couch in my sewing room, in his pajama pants and reading.

"It's not that late, is it?" I asked checking my watch.

"No. I just felt like getting ready for bed early and reading."

"Oh. Okay." I sat down next to him.

"How are you feeling?" he asked, brushing my hair away from my forehead.

"Okay. Better."

"Not scared?"

"Well, I was scared when it was happening, but like I said, that's normal."

"Good." He reached over and gently kissed me.

My heart pounded against my chest as I kissed him back. I so wanted to be with him.

"I love you so much, Sid."

"Lisa, I love you."

We said good night somewhat later and with a great deal of reluctance. After changing and washing up, I got into bed and knew nothing more until Sid nudged me awake. He was dressed to go running.

"You slept through your alarm again." His tone chided, but he was smiling.

I blinked. "I slept through the night. That's two nights in a row, Sid."

He grinned. "That's good. Now, get up. We don't want to get any further behind today."

It was a normal morning. Shortly after we got to the offices, the pagers went off.

"My turn," said Sid.

It was a pickup down near the port of Los Angeles. Sid was gone for a couple hours, and I went back to working on some edits for one of his financial articles. As I put the printout on his desk, however, I found the file I'd been looking for.

"Shavings!" I yelped. It was for a back cover piece I was doing for a sewing magazine. Worse yet, the essay was due in the magazine offices the next day.

"I'm back," Sid announced from my office.

I went in there with the file. "I found it. I must have left this on your desk sometime last week and forgotten I had. And guess what? Due in their offices tomorrow. It never fails."

"What? Your sewing essay? You'll get it done in plenty of time." He gently tugged me to his chest and kissed me.

I giggled. "You can't keep doing that. That's probably why I left that file on your desk, you know."

"Okay. Back to work we go. Oh, uh, the drop won't happen until four-thirty, but I'll have to leave by three-thirty."

"Okay."

I ate lunch in the office but got the essay ready for review by one.

As Sid made his notes on it, we got a call on the Quickline phone. Sid answered it, then put them on hold and looked at me.

"Someone upline wants a meeting."

"About what?" I asked.

"Don't know. They're asking for Thursday. How about two p.m. at the Code Five?"

The Code Five (not the real name) was a diner near the airport which handled things like film to develop and paychecks and was an occasional safe house.

"Sounds good."

Sid set up the meeting, then went back to marking up my essay. When he was done, I took the printout back into my office. I stood next to my desk, reading the notes, then reading the essay again. Sid came out of office behind me. I bent to make a note on my desktop. Sid's hands slid under my jacket and up to my breasts. He gently pulled me back closer to him.

"Oh, Sid. That really feels nice, but..." I was getting irritated.

"Too far?"

"Uh. I've got work to do." I turned and faced him.

"I'm sorry." He smiled. "You were just kind of tempting there and I wanted to try giving in to it for a change."

I sighed and gave him a quick kiss. "It's okay, I guess. I've got to get this done though and I don't have a lot of time before I have to head over to the overnight office to get this sent."

"Okay." He wasn't thrilled and it looked like he was going to say something else, but he didn't.

"I'll probably be gone when you get back. I've got league tonight and Bible Study, so I'll just stay out and pick up dinner somewhere."

"You want to go out?"

"I don't want to miss any more games and, yeah, I do want to go to Bible Study." I hoped I didn't sound as irritated as I felt.

Sid sighed but backed off.

I had the essay corrected in time for Sid to take off. I kissed him goodbye, then set up the letter quality printer. While the article and the cover letter printed, I went and changed clothes. It was ten minutes to four when I got to the overnight company office and got the article sent in time to get to the magazine the next morning.

I ate dinner at a small restaurant nearby, then headed to the gym. Sid didn't show, at least, not while I was there. He'd buzzed my pager at a quarter to five, so I knew he was home. After Bible Study, Frank, Esther, Kathy, Jesse, and I went out for a drink. I called Sid to let him know and invited him to come. He declined. I thought he sounded like he was a little peeved.

It turned out that he was. When I came in through the garage, he was there, in pajama bottoms and robe.

"You do not look happy," I said, heading for my room.

"I'm not. Why didn't you come home after Bible Study?"

"Because I wanted to go out with my friends. I did invite you."

"I wasn't dressed to go out and by the time I would have been, you'd be back."

There was an awkward pause.

"Alright," I said. "I'm going to get dressed for bed."

Sid followed me into the sewing room. He already had the couch set up and a book lying next to it.

"I'll be out in a minute," I told him.

"Thanks."

After I changed, we kissed each other goodnight. Later, the nightmare came back with a vengeance. Sid was there, rubbing my back, as I gasped and got myself under control.

"I'm never going to get over these," I sniffed.

"Yes, you will. They will fade with time, maybe not completely, but they will fade." He laid his head against mine. "Listen, I'm sorry about earlier today. When we were necking last night, it got me pretty stirred up, and then temptation struck, and since things have changed between us, I thought maybe I could have a little fun."

"Sid, I didn't mind you grabbing a feel. I was worried about that story, and you kissed me, and then you wanted to play games, and I did not want to miss my deadline. I don't want to make you feel like I don't want to be touched or anything. I just didn't think you were listening to me."

He sighed. "I wasn't. But you're not really listening to me, either. It seems like as soon as we eat dinner, you're rushing off to a meeting or have something else you want to do, and I'm not really part of it."

"I want my life to be normal again."

"Yeah, but your life includes me. At least, I hope it does."

"Shavings," I grumbled. "I screwed up, didn't I?"

"And I didn't realize until tonight that I'm having another problem, too."

I looked at him. "What?"

"I'm bored. I am bored out of my skull. I seriously considered meeting you at your bible study tonight, that's how bored I am."

"But, Sid, you have your music. You have reading, even some TV."

"I have a lot more time on my hands than I used to."

I suddenly realized that he was right. Before, he'd be out anywhere from three to six nights a week, and sometimes all day on Saturdays.

"So, how do I fill all those hours formerly filled with the pursuit of carnal pleasure?" He smiled at me, sheepishly. "I was hoping to spend more of it with you. I understand how you feel about being glued to my hip, and I really do not want to do the clingy thing, even if you wanted me, too."

"Which I do not." I looked down at my hands.

"Good. But, Lisa, you are very important to me, and I like being around you. I love talking to you, and teasing you, and you teasing me, and the way we verbally spar sometimes. And then when we get close, like we are right now." He shook his head. "I love you so much, Lisa."

I bumped up against him. "I love being around you, too, Sid. We'll just have to figure it out." I touched his cheek. "I do like being in the library with you, even when I'm reading or knitting."

"I kinda like that, too. But we could use a little more variety."

"And you could use a hobby. How about charity work?"

He nodded. "That might be something."

He got up and bent over to kiss me. He sighed deeply, then I slid down under my covers and slept through until morning.

April 10, 1985

S id had an odd grin on his face when I came to breakfast that morning.

"How close are we to not being behind?" he asked me as I yawned and piled fruit salad on my plate.

I blinked and thought. "I think we're mostly caught up, or at least, on track. Why?"

"Nothing." He buried his face into the morning newspaper. He flipped a corner down. "Yet."

I was too tired to wonder at it. He finished before I did, and I offered to bring the dishes back into the kitchen. When I got to my office, he was there waiting.

"Alright," I said. "I'm more awake. What's up?"

"I know we talked after your nightmare last night," he said leaning his backside on the front of my desk. "But I had an odd little revelation in the shower this morning."

I folded my arms in front of myself. "Okay."

"Yesterday, I was pretty horny, and I was pretty P.O.'d at you. Now, not too long ago, the first thing I would do was go out to a bar, whatever, and get myself laid."

"I'm assuming you didn't last night."

"The thought never occurred to me." He put his hand on my forearm. "Lisa, that's what I've been waiting for. The signal that I really am done with sleeping around. Believe me, that combination of being hot for your bod and totally annoyed with you used to send me running for tail faster than just about anything else, especially these past few months, when I was really trying not to. Last night, I was wonderfully stirred up and really angry that you weren't there. And I never even thought about going and getting laid. All I wanted was you."

"I'm glad," I said, not quite getting what he was saying.

He laughed softly. "Lisa, I'm ready. I am ready to promise a lifetime commitment to you and my fidelity. And I am not going to wait to do it. We can't afford to take that chance. Right here, right now, I promise to be with you for the rest of our lives and to stay faithful to you and you only."

The bottom dropped out. "Oh. Sid."

I flew into his arms and we kissed.

"Sid," I gasped when I could. "I promise, too. I will be with you for the rest of our lives, and I will be faithful."

He pulled away for a moment. "I have something for you. Um. When I had that diamond reset last summer into your necklace, I bought the earrings I gave you last Christmas, and something else, too."

He handed me a ring box. I almost choked. Sid had given me a beautiful necklace of diamonds and aquamarines, my birthstone, then the earrings. I didn't wear bracelets, so I'd figured that wasn't coming.

"It is technically a dinner ring," he said. "To go with the other pieces. You don't have to wear it on your left hand. But I can't think of a better time to give it to you."

The ring followed the same motif of a round-cut gem surrounded by smaller ones of the other color. My necklace had two such circles suspended from the s-chain. The top circle was an aquamarine, surrounded by tiny diamonds. The bottom had a diamond surrounded by aquamarines. My earrings were the same. The ring had an aquamarine at its center, surrounded by tiny diamonds.

"It's beautiful, Sid." I couldn't believe what I was doing, but I pulled the ring from the box and slid it onto my right ring finger. Or tried to.

Sid frowned. "I had that sized to that wedding set we use."

Sid and I have wedding rings that we wear when we're posing as a married couple. I put the ring on my left ring finger. It fit perfectly.

"My right hand is slightly larger than my left," I told him.

He put his hand over mine. "You don't have to wear it full-time if you don't want to."

I pulled my hand away and admired the sparkling gems. "I won't, but... I kind of like this."

"Let's call it a promise ring, then."

I giggled. "Like we're in high school."

"Oh, I hope we're past that." Sid's gorgeous blue eyes danced like the sparkles in my ring.

I kissed him again. He put his hand on my cheek, then pulled away.

"You know what else this means?" he asked me, his voice taking on a rich, earthy tone. "With your permission, of course, then tonight is going to be our night."

"Can we afford to wait?"

He shifted with a slightly uncomfortable hiss. "Let's give you some time to get used to the idea. Besides, I want this to be extra special. Let me romance you. Dinner, maybe dancing, and then you and me."

"Oh, Sid." Blushing, I kissed him, then just looked into his so very sweet eyes. "You think we could eventually get married, too? It would make things easier at church."

"Sure. Why not?"

I had a bad feeling we were going to be behind again, but I didn't care. He held me and we kissed deeply and richly. I knew Sid had a point about letting me get used to the idea that we were really going to be having sex for the first time. My first time. I trusted him to take good care of me, and I couldn't help but be delighted that he found such joy in it.

It had been Sid's promise, also, that when we came together, it would be in joy, or it would not happen. I was definitely feeling the joy, and a lot of other wonderful, delicious feelings.

So was he. We held each other, kissing and kissing, our tongues intertwining. His hands wandered delightfully, and I couldn't help but gasp with how good it felt.

Then the phone rang.

I have no idea how Sid managed it. He would answer the phone no matter what state his was in or with whom. He still had that skill. Somehow, without his lips leaving mine, he got the phone off the hook and the speakerphone on, then moved away and said, "Hello?"

"Sid, it's Beth Carpatti."

Sid kissed my forehead. "Good to hear from you, Beth. How's it going?"

He began kissing my mouth again.

"Pretty awful. I have AIDS."

Sid stopped cold.

"I'm so sorry," he said, melting away from me.

"I'm pretty sure it was that loser drug addict that I connected with after our fling last summer. But the doctor said I should contact all my partners."

"Of course," Sid gasped, but then did something that made me love him all the more. "How are you doing?"

"It's awful." Beth sounded like she was crying. "I just want to be alone right now."

"Sure. I'll check in later."

The phone buzzed with the dial tone. Sid did manage to switch off the speakerphone. He also got up and went to the other side of the room from me.

"Sid," I whispered.

"Do you have any idea how close we just came?" he said, his face ashen.

"Sid, she's not sure it was you."

"I have come this close to infecting you."

"You haven't done a damned thing!" I glared at him. "Why don't you check in with the doctor?"

Sid nodded. He went into his office, where his phone book was, flipped to a specific page and dialed.

"Is Dr. Kline available?" he told the person on the other end. "I have a bit of an emergency."

Dr. Kline agreed to see Sid that day if he could get there in forty minutes or so. Sid agreed, and I did not want to think what it would take to get from the house in Beverly Hills to the office near Cedars Sinai Medical Center, at the western end of the really trendy part of Melrose Avenue. I insisted on driving because he was in no shape to, and we managed to get there in twenty-five minutes. We still had to wait another hour or so before the nurse called Sid back to the exam room.

Sadly, I could not go in with Sid. I sat in the waiting room, reading old People magazines and a few pamphlets on various health care issues. One pamphlet I made a point of putting in my purse. When Sid finally emerged, carrying his suit jacket, but otherwise perfect, I went up to him.

"I have to get some blood drawn," he said. "We can talk about the rest when we're done."

He did seem a lot more relaxed than he had when he'd gone into Dr. Kline's exam room. He was still shook, of course, but no longer panicking.

The sweet young thing that drew Sid's blood was exactly the kind of cutie that Sid had loved to mess with.

"Are you going to be okay?" Sid asked her as he rolled up the sleeve to his shirt.

"I have stuck so many of you boys this past month and have been fine. I'm not worried." she replied, never mind that she put on an extra pair of rubber gloves.

As she pulled together paperwork and vials, she gave me a look.

"So, is this your sister?" she asked Sid.

"Uh, no," Sid said, then looked at me. He put his hand out and I grasped it. "This is my... Girlfriend."

It was the first time either of us had acknowledged it.

The lab tech's eyebrows rose.

"It's something new," Sid said, even though she was obviously wondering how straight Sid was.

The lab tech shrugged. Okay, she also looked at Sid with unguarded lust, too, but that neither surprised me nor bothered me. Sid's eyes drifted toward me. I squeezed his hand.

We were done in a few minutes, and the lab tech placed a ball of cotton over the small prick and taped it down. Sid kept his hand on it for the full five minutes as we walked back to my truck. While I unlocked the passenger door, Sid put his jacket back on.

"You seem calmer," I said as I started the engine.

"Well, there's good news, bad news." Sid took a deep breath. "Dr. Kline said she likes my odds. Apparently, only one percent of cases are from heterosexual contact, and since Beth does have a probable source of infection which occurred after her contact with me, if I have it, I probably did not get it from her. But I did get the lecture on my sex habits." He glanced at me. "Former sex habits. Also, I don't have any symptoms, which is a good sign, but hardly conclusive."

"I've heard it can take years for symptoms to show."

"Exactly. That's why we had to get the blood drawn. There's a new test for the virus that causes AIDS." He sighed. "We should know in a few days."

"Good. Why don't we go to lunch and try to relax, and then we can talk things through some more when we get home."

"Yeah. That sounds good." Sid took a deep breath and let it out.

I braked for a red light, then looked over at him. "Sid, I want you to know this does not affect the promise I made to you this morning."

"I'm glad." He reached over and put his hand over mine where it rested on the gear shift. "It doesn't affect mine, either. Not in the least."

I called Conchetta from the restaurant to let her know we were eating lunch out and asked her to save what she'd made, and we'd eat it for dinner that night.

When we got home, I got Sid settled on the living room couch and just held him for several minutes.

"You know," I said finally. "I did find a pamphlet on AIDS and how to deal with it. It was clearly directed at gay men, but guys doing the penetrating are not at as high a risk."

"Which reminds me. I didn't get to tell you the bad news," he said, gazing unseeing at the floor. "No sex for us until I'm clear."

"That's only for a few days. I can wait."

"And if I have it, I may have already infected you."

That took my breath away for a moment.

"It's body fluids, Lisa. Saliva."

"We don't know that you have it, Sid."

"Yeah, but the way we've been kissing lately, there's been a lot of fluid exchanging. Dr. Kline said that it's only possible that saliva can cause infection. They don't know one way or another yet. But she said she hasn't seen any real evidence that it does. That's the worst of it." Sid seemed to cave into himself. "It's bad enough thinking I might have a fatal disease. It's worse thinking that I gave it to you. That's the part that kills me. That I hurt you."

"You didn't know. Nobody did." I sighed. "It's not like you did it intentionally. And again, we don't know that you are even infected yet. If you find out you are, I'll get tested, and if I've got it, too, then we'll deal with it then. And like you said, the odds are overwhelmingly in our favor."

He looked at me. "You're not mad at me? As much as you hated me fooling around, I would think you'd be furious about this."

"Maybe it hasn't hit me yet." I touched his face. "I don't know. All that just doesn't seem important right now. It's in the past. Right?"

"Yeah."

I reached over to kiss his mouth, and he pulled back.

"Sid, if you have the virus, and if it can be transmitted through saliva, it's already too late."

I reached again. He hesitated, then kissed me with his lips closed, but slowly they opened, and he kissed me again.

Then we just held each other until it grew dark outside. Dinner was subdued and Sid picked at his chicken salad. We sat in the library together and held each other again. I went first to get dressed for bed and as I left my bathroom, I made another decision. I went through the house to Sid's bedroom and knocked on his door.

"Come on in," he said with a sigh. "I'm covered."

He was wearing his pajama bottoms and sitting on the edge of his bed.

"If you don't mind," I said softly. "I'd like to spend the night in here."

"Why?" he asked.

I shrugged. "It just seems like the thing to do."

He nodded and got in bed. I slid under the covers next to him and kissed him good night.

Some hours later, I woke up. Sid's sleepy chatter grew more and more anxious.

"Robinson," he called, as he lay on his side facing away from me. "Robinson, no!"

His eyes opened as he gasped for air. I rubbed his back.

"I'm here, Sid. It was just a dream."

His breathing slowed and he rolled onto his back. I reached for him, and he pulled away.

"It's okay," I told him.

"No, it's not okay. I feel so contaminated." He looked at me. "That's why you're here right now, isn't it?"

"It is." I smiled at him. "You told me last fall I'm not the only one who has nightmares. I'm happy to return the favor."

He sighed and looked up at the ceiling. "I dream about my first kill, too."

He meant the first time he'd killed someone. Sid having fought in Vietnam and given the way people were prone to shooting at us, it was inevitable that we'd both killed people. I'd killed my first the previous summer, which was when my nightmares started. He seldom talked about his experiences in Vietnam but had told me bits and pieces here and there.

"Do you want to talk about it?"

"Actually, I already have." He took a deep breath and let it out. "Now, that I think about it, a couple of times. Well, hinted at it, anyway."

"How do you mean?"

He shook his head. "It's not important now." He took another deep breath. "It was near the start of my tour, and I was in a pretty bad way. We'd go out on patrol for three weeks at a time, and I kept getting so horny. Three weeks without sex and obviously the stress of not knowing when we'd come under fire. Nothing helped. Near the end of the third patrol, I was really a mess. I snuck out of camp that evening to get myself off, not that it was going to do any good, mind you. But I was desperate, and stupidly, I left my gun in the camp. I figured I'd be back in no time. I was just getting started when I heard the gunfire. A VC sniper took out Robinson and a couple others. The weird thing was, I was almost on top of the sniper, but hadn't seen him because I was too anxious to get my rocks off. And I didn't have my gun. I did have my knife and charged the sniper, knocked his rifle out of the way. He came back at me, and I stuck the knife in his belly and then watched as he bled." Sid swallowed. "When I got back to camp, all I wanted to do was wash the blood off my hands. Robinson was dead and I could have saved him if I'd just been paying attention."

"And now you've got blood on your hands again."

He nodded.

"I don't know if I would have understood that before last summer, but I do now." I wanted so badly to touch him, to gather him into my arms and hold him. "We both know intellectually that if you have AIDS, you did not do it to me or to yourself. It just happened. And we both know it's really hard to look at these things intellectually when we're worried, hurt, and scared. But as you've told me, sometimes that's what we must hold onto. In the meantime, I'm here for life, Sid."

"I just hope we have more time."

"We run that risk every day. They were shooting at us last Monday."

"Too true." Sid slowly rolled onto his side and faced me. "I guess we'll deal with it, then." He sighed. "I hope you don't mind waiting to make love."

"I've been waiting all my life. What's a few extra days?" I thought of something else. "You know that pamphlet said we could use a condom."

Sid snorted. "No way. I conceived Nick wearing a condom. Trust me, they are not foolproof by any means. I know of at least one abortion that I caused with a leaky one, and it's always possible that Nick has an older sibling out there that we don't know about yet." He shuddered. "That's why the first thing I did when I got my money was get my surgery."

I smiled. "We could look at this as if we're waiting for the biopsy results on a lump."

"There's one major distinction, though. I can't give you cancer. Sleeping with me will not give you cancer."

"I'm not likely to get AIDS, either. The odds are in our favor."

Sid smiled and reached his hand to touch my face. "And you don't mind kissing me?"

I went ahead and showed him that I didn't.

April 11-13, 1985

No surprise, at our appointment that morning, Dr. Heilland was pretty interested in Sid's status with the AIDS virus, although mostly in how we were dealing with it.

"You're not trying to hide any angry feelings, Lisa?" he asked.

I frowned. "I don't think so."

"Lisa's not one for hiding her feelings," Sid said, looking at me.

I shifted, oddly uncomfortable for a change. The weird thing was, we never did talk about the trauma I'd been dealing with. Sid did spend a few minutes talking to Dr. Heilland alone while I used the rest room.

From Dr. Heilland's, we went to our meeting at the Code Five diner.

"How are you feeling?" I asked Sid.

He winced. "Getting used to things."

"I know." I groaned. "Things were feeling pretty normal for a while. Now, it's all weird again."

"We'll work it out."

At the diner, the owner saw us coming and pointed us to a booth in the back corner. A lone man sat in the end seat, watching the door. It wasn't entirely possible to say how tall he was, but he didn't look any bigger than average height. He was balding and his remaining hair was brown and neatly clipped. His suit was a nice solid gray lightweight wool. I sighed as we walked toward the table. There was French Dip sandwich on special that day and it didn't look too likely I'd get one.

Sid let me scoot into the booth first, then sat down next to me.

"Big Red," the man said, shaking my hand. "Little Red." He shook Sid's.

"I'm Little Red," I said through my teeth.

"Call me Clive," he said, adding the specific division of the CIA that he was with. "Heard our friend Danschenko gave you a little present."

"He sure did," said Sid. "Kind of a sick joke, too. First, he hides a microdot in the jar, then sends one of your guys to go through our trash to find it."

"It wasn't one of our guys. It was one of the Colombians."

"What?" I snapped.

Sid's hand landed on my thigh as a reminder to keep cool. I took a deep breath.

"Alright," Sid said, far more coolly than I could have. "What do you know about the Colombians and Danschenko?"

Clive sighed. "Danny boy has been walking the fence for us for years. Well, thanks to Gorbachev and all the changes in the Soviet Union, he wants to defect, which will not make his bosses back home happy at all. So, he's playing everybody he knows against everyone else, hoping that in the chaos, his butt will be covered. He set up the kidnapping with the Colombians, then told me that he needed the van and the safe house to help a couple of his colleagues defect."

"And you bought it," said Sid.

"Not entirely." Clive shrugged. "I don't trust Danny boy any further than I can throw him. But, yeah, it seemed legit until I found out the Colombians were in town. That's when I knew they had targeted the Martinez kid. The good thing was she'd joined your church youth group like I told her to."

"Joined...?" I gaped and looked at Sid.

Sid glared at Clive. "You know who we are."

"Of course, I do. I've been working with Red Knight for years and I know the plan."

Red Knight is Henry's code name.

"The plan," Sid repeated.

"You don't have Need to Know yet."

Sid's hand squeezed my thigh, and it was a good thing, too. I was about to bounce out of my seat and throttle Clive.

Clive waved Sid off. "In any case, when we set up the kid and her mother here, I told her to join the church group for an extra layer of security."

"It would have nice to know that," I said through my teeth.

"It worked out."

Sid looked at Clive curiously. "When did you find out the Colombians had gotten the wrong target?"

"After I'd gotten my butt kicked for helping the kidnappers." Clive rolled his eyes. "It's a good thing your girl here is as good as Red Knight said she is. Once she got out, we were able to call local law enforcement."

"As I understood it, they got the kidnappers." Sid's eyes narrowed. "How is it that they're still on the loose?"

Clive chuckled. "Medellín has some really good lawyers and plenty of cash. They surrendered their passports, not that it will keep them here, and everyone knows it. If they're still in the country, it's because they're trying to take out Danschenko. They seem to think he screwed them."

"Such a surprise," I grumbled, then suddenly remembered something. "When Danschenko gave us that caviar, he said something about us having had a traumatic week." I glared at Clive. "He knew I'd gotten kidnapped. Does he know we're operatives?"

"I don't think so." Clive shrugged as if he didn't care either way.

Sid looked at him carefully. "If he does know, how will that affect the plan? I'm assuming you and your friends don't want our covers blown."

"Good question." Clive nodded and smiled. "Of course, we don't want your covers blown. As to what Danny knows about you two, I have no idea. But I wouldn't worry about him."

"So why are we here?" Sid asked.

Clive shifted. "Just wanted to check in with you guys. Danny's in the wind at the moment."

"We saw him last Monday." Sid glanced at me. "The Colombians came calling."

"He made it out. Will you let me know if he contacts you? We want to help."

I snorted.

Clive glared at me. "You think you know so much?"

"I know about being held hostage for five days when you knew where I was and wouldn't do anything. Funny how you're friends with both Danschenko and Medillín."

Clive shifted again. "You domestic types. You don't get squat what we have to do in the field. Yeah. We make friends with people we don't like because we have to." He glared at Sid. "You were in country. You should know what that's like."

"Yes," said Sid, his voice taking on that angry edge. "But I also know the ends don't always justify the means."

I pressed my lips together. Sid looked over at me, then leaned forward and sent Clive a truly menacing glare.

"She's on a bit of a hair trigger." Sid gestured my way. "As I'm sure you can imagine. It might be fun to trip it and see what she does to you."

Clive sent me a glance, then got up. "Let me know if Danny gets in touch."

He left.

I let out the breath I'd been holding. Sid looked at me.

"They've got French Dip on special." I squirmed. "Can we stay?"

He sighed. "Sure."

I waved the owner over and ordered my sandwich with cole slaw instead of fries. Sid had a salad.

"I wonder what he wants." I fidgeted with the saltshaker.

"Clive?" Sid looked out the door thoughtfully. "My guess is that whatever was in that jar of caviar, it was not what they expected. Or they think Danschenko is holding out on them."

"That makes sense." I smiled at him. "Nice bit with the hair trigger."

"Yeah." He looked away.

"I hope I looked menacing enough."

"Oh, you did."

"Oh, no. I'm sorry."

"It's alright, honey." He put his hand on mine. "We're both under a lot of stress right now."

I nodded. Sid had gone back to closed-mouth kisses that morning, which didn't feel at all good, although I had teased him into one really good one right before we'd left for Dr. Heilland's.

When we got back to the house, Henry called. Sid went over our meeting with Clive, then Henry told him what had been on the micro-dot: a list of known U.S. operatives in the Soviet Union and Eastern Europe.

"Good lord, Sid," I said when he'd repeated the conversation. "Where did Danschenko get that?"

"He presumably stole it and is now offering it to the CIA probably as a sign of good faith."

"But if the list is wrong or purposely misleading it could nobble a lot of good agents."

Sid nodded. "There is an appalling lack of trust on all sides."

"Well, you can hardly blame them." I sat back in my desk chair. "Now what?"

Sid shrugged. "Not much we can do."

I went back to focusing on writing work. It did help steady me in one sense. Sid seemed to be feeling a little better after giving Clive some grief.

Then later that afternoon, I went into the rumpus room to find a book and found Conchetta dusting in there. She was wearing a Twisted Sister t-shirt and looked unhappy.

"You okay?" I asked.

She sighed. "He told me about the AIDS."

"It's not for sure yet." I shrugged. "Conchetta, if something happens to Sid, I'll still keep you on."

"I know. I'm not worried about that." She glared at the shelf for a moment, then left the room.

I couldn't help smiling. Conchetta was very firm that she did not want to be friends with us. Too many times, she'd been called a friend by an employer only to be fired soon after. Yet, she clearly cared deeply about Sid, as if he were a surrogate son. [She cared about you, too. – SEH]

As Sid and I finished dinner that evening, I sighed.

"Sid, you know what you said on Tuesday about me rushing off to do whatever without taking you into account?"

"Yes?"

"Well, I'm a little stuck. I've got to sew the buttons on Kathy's dress tonight. Esther and I are taking her out for a bachelorette party tomorrow. I think I told you about that, didn't I?"

"I think so."

"Anyway, I have to have the buttons done tonight so that I can pin the hem in on her on Saturday, and there are a lot of buttons."

He looked at me sadly. "Lisa, you don't have to treat me like cut crystal."

"No. It's not that." I sighed. "It's that I have been running off to do my own thing and I don't want to do that, and…" I bit my lip. "I'm just not sure how to take you into account, especially in terms of commitments I've already made. I don't want to ask permission."

"That would not be good."

"No, it wouldn't."

Sid sighed and thought about it. "We'll have to keep talking about what's going on, then, I guess. Are you going to be holed up in your sewing room all night?"

"It's hand sewing, and it will probably take all night. But I don't have to be in my sewing room."

On the other hand, that is exactly where we landed, on the couch, no less. I stitched away while Sid, who had already changed to his pajama bottoms, read to me, his feet in my lap, underneath the dress as I worked on it. We both agreed it was a decidedly pleasant way to spend the evening, and it did a lot to help us both finally relax.

However, when I invited him into my bedroom to sleep with me, he shook his head.

"It's not the disease thing," he said. "At least, I don't think so." His hand cupped my face. "But it is getting... Physically painful to lie next to you and not make love. And it's not anything you're doing. Just human anatomy, is all."

I nodded, then kissed him goodnight. At least, he opened his mouth that time.

I had one nightmare and Sid was there. Then I went back to sleep, only to wake up soon after. Sid was yelling in his sleep. I hurried out to the sewing room, rubbing his back as he awoke. He tried pushing away, but I held on and he slowly relaxed.

It was in the middle of the next morning that things really, really got weird.

I could hear Sid on the phone in his office, but couldn't hear what he said, which was just as well, as it was my turn to write a first draft of one of the articles we were working on together. A few minutes later, Sid came out of the office.

"We did talk about Nick coming down this weekend, didn't we?" he asked.

"Yeah. He's coming for Darby's birthday party on Sunday," I glanced up from the computer screen, then finished a sentence.

"I was just talking with Rachel's friend, Marlou Parks? She called to verify the flight times and told me that she'd be at the airport to pick Nick up when he gets back. She set it up so that he can fly alone."

I sat back in my chair. "That's interesting."

"Yeah. She even said that she knew there was some bad blood between me and Rachel but asked that I not judge her too harshly."

"It's too late for that one," I grumbled.

Sid shrugged. "The question is, do we trust her?"

I thought back to when I'd seen her. "She didn't seem flaky to me. And Nick really likes her."

"There is that."

"Why don't we see what Nick has to say when he gets here?"

"Sounds good." Then Sid dropped his bomb. "So, what do we tell him about us?"

"What do you mean?"

"If we're getting married, that affects him as much as it does us."

"Married?" I gasped. I'd forgotten that I'd suggested that. "Um. Are we?"

Sid stepped back, looking terrified.

"No!" I yelped. "Sid…"

"Don't you want to be with me?" The fear in his eyes seared me to the bone.

I stood and went to him. "Sid, being with you is all I want. When I said for life, I meant it and I still do."

"But you wanted to get married to make it easier with the church thing."

"I know," I squeaked.

"So, what gives?"

I took a deep breath. "I don't think I'm ready to tell anyone yet."

Sid suddenly burst into laughter. "Really?"

"I do not even want to think about what Janet and Sylvia will do," I said, my voice dull and flat.

"Okay. Point taken."

I put my hands on his chest. "Look, Sid, my commitment to you is sound. I want you and no one else. Getting used to marrying you. I'm shocked, but that one's a little harder."

He pressed his lips to my forehead. "Okay. I can live with that. But what do we tell Nick? And what about why you are not currently in my bedroom at night?"

"You mean the AIDS thing?"

"Yeah."

I closed my eyes. "That would be pretty hard on a kid, especially since we don't know whether you have it or not. And we do have a good excuse in terms of my morals for why I'm not there."

Sid looked at me for a moment, as if he wanted to ask something else, but let it go.

I swallowed, then felt my spirit lift. "Here's an idea. We need to know if Nick can keep a secret, right?"

"Well, that would make it easier to take custody, yes."

"Why don't we tell him that we are going to get married, but don't want to tell anyone yet."

"As in we don't want people to pressure us into wedding plans when we're not yet ready for that."

"Which is the truth, really."

Sid nuzzled me behind my ear. "That is a good idea."

"Thanks."

That having been settled, I went back to my first draft. But that did not mean that my innards were any the quieter.

Nick, when he came out of the tunnel at LAX that afternoon, was filled with his usual happy energy. He hugged Sid, then gave me an extra-long hug. I buried my face in the curly, dark hair so much like his father's.

"I'm so glad to see you, Nick," I said, feeling some loosening of the tension that had surrounded Sid and me for that day.

The bachelorette party that night was a lot of fun, too. Sid had already taken Nick out to dinner and to go see a movie when Esther picked me up in her aging Lincoln. We picked up Sarah Williams, then got Kathy, and had dinner in Santa Monica. Kathy had a bad feeling she knew where we were headed after that. Her fears were well-founded. It was one of the nicer male strip joints in Venice Beach.

Both she and Sarah were properly scandalized, but soon settled in and had a good time. There was no reason not to. They don't strip all the way and when you can't take it anymore, you don't look. Okay, we all got a little embarrassed. Esther said it reminded her of the time she'd caught Frank trying to get to the bathroom with only his undershorts on. I was the coolest of the bunch. Esther called me on it.

"It's a little embarrassing," I said after the show. "But this is a piece of cake compared to the first time I came here."

Sarah laughed. "You? At a strip show?"

"It gets worse," I said. "Sid brought me."

The other women gaped.

"I was having one of my blue days and he was trying to cheer me up." I made a point of hiding my smile behind a sip of wine.

It had been a very special night, a couple weeks before my birthday. We'd had an exceptionally bad fight the night after Valentine's Day, and it had seemed like the impasse in our relationship could never be resolved.

"I don't think I could handle Dan being here with me," Sarah said.

"Frank would be fun." Esther raised her hand for the waiter. "The biggest problem would be keeping him from joining the dancers." She grinned. "He looks pretty good in his undershorts." Her face suddenly fell.

Sarah reached over and patted her hand. "It's okay, Esther. It will all work out."

Kathy and I stared at Sarah and Esther.

Esther made a face. "So, Sarah and I had a little talk not too long ago. Remind me not to get drunk around her again."

"You weren't drunk," Sarah said.

"I don't want to talk about guys, anyway." Esther looked again for the waiter. "What does it take to get a drink around here?"

I was glad Esther didn't want to continue the conversation. Sid and I were long past our impasse. I wondered when he would hear from the doctor. I suppose it was possible the test would come back positive, but I didn't want to think about that. I didn't want to think about the weirdness of that morning and how scared Sid had been when he'd thought I didn't want him. And I really didn't want to think about how deliciously tingly I felt at the thought of finally sleeping with him.

It didn't help when he kissed me after his nightmare that night, and again when he kissed me after mine.

We were pretty worn out that morning when we got up. Over breakfast, Nick was full of chatter about the movie they'd seen the night before and what he and Sid were going to do that day. Nick had picked up an interest in baseball after spending a week or so at a baseball camp the summer before. So, Sid had gotten tickets to the Dodgers game that evening. They were playing the San Francisco Giants, and Nick was excited to see the Dodgers' hot pitching ace, Fernando Valenzuela, and pelted us with batting averages and earned runs and how he was really a Giants fan, but Valenzuela was really, really good.

Sid smiled gently at me. He is not a sports fan, per se. He likes sports and can talk about them because that's what guys talk about. As he once put it, he prefers indoor activities and playing rather than watching. I caught my breath again. Sid chuckled.

He and I had already talked about my plans for the day, so when we were done eating, I went back to my sewing room to work on projects and get things ready for Kathy. I heard the phone ring around ten, but since it was Sid's line, I ignored it. Sid knocked on my door some minutes later.

"Come on in," I said, frowning over the pattern instructions for a pair of dress slacks with an asymmetrical flap for the front opening.

Sid shut the door behind him. In the rumpus room, Nick was listening to his new Tears for Fears album on the stereo.

"That was Dr. Kline," Sid said softly.

I swallowed. "And...?"

"Good news, bad news." Sid leaned against the cutting table. "My test came back negative."

"Oh, thank you, Jesus!"

Sid put up his hands. "It's not time to celebrate yet. The problem is, they don't entirely know how long it takes after infection for the virus to show up in the blood stream. Since the test was released, they're getting better data, but they don't really know yet. And it hasn't even been a full month since my last contact. So, Dr. Kline wants to test me again in six months, and for me to assume I can still spread it until then."

"In other words, we're not going to be doing anything for a while."

"Nope." He grimaced. "Not to mention the enthralling fun of living in limbo for six months."

"Yuck." I went over and pulled him into my arms. "We'll manage."

He held me tightly. "Yeah."

I looked over at the rumpus room. "Should we tell Nick?"

"I don't think so. We don't know anything yet and I don't want him worrying about me. It's a lot for a kid to be carrying around."

"I don't think I want to tell my family yet, either." I frowned. "About anything about us right now. There's just too much up in the air. I mean, Daddy's figured out you're with me for the duration."

"Honey, he'd figured that out a couple years ago." Sid pressed his lips to my forehead. "Listen, I'd better get back to Nick."

"Okay."

Kathy arrived at three. She crowed over the dress again and all those buttons. I went to work on pinning in the hem and was just about done when Sid and Nick came into the sewing room.

"Lisa—" Sid stopped. "Where are you?"

"Down here." I said through the pins in my mouth. I was lying on my side, pushing the last bit of silk taffeta into place.

"Wow, Kathy. You look great!" Nick yelled.

"Thank you, Nick." Kathy said. "Don't you think Lisa did a good job, Sid?"

"A very good job. Uh, Lisa, Nick wants to see batting practice, so we're heading out to the stadium, now."

"Have a good time, guys."

Kathy looked at herself in the mirror. "Fernando pitching tonight?"

"Yep," Nick said.

Kathy suddenly gasped. "Young man, is that a Giants' cap I see you wearing?"

Nick laughed. "They're my team."

"Uh-huh. I see that we are going to have knock some sense into you."

"And I root for the 'Niners, too!" Nick blew a raspberry at her and ran off as Sid laughed.

"We'll see you soon, Kathy. See you tonight, Lisa."

"See you later."

There was an awkward pause, then I slid the last pin into place.

"I think I've got it." I pulled the extra pins from my mouth and jammed then into the pin cushion on my wrist.

"It looks beautiful, Lisa." Kathy gazed into the mirror. "I can't thank you enough."

"Will you hold still? I want to be sure I've got it."

The hem was level. I unbuttoned the dress and Kathy slid out of it. As she got dressed in her regular clothes, I hung the dress up on a hangar and put it on its peg.

"Lisa, what's going on?"

"I'm fine, Kathy." I fluffed the skirt on the wedding dress a little.

"No, you're not," she said softly. She glanced at the dress. "Is it the wedding bothering you?"

"No." I snorted. "Not in the least."

"Your wedding?"

"Assuming there is one." I blinked and shook my head.

"Sid doesn't seem like he's against the idea."

"He's not. But it's not that simple." I sank into my sewing chair and began weeping full out. "We found out on Wednesday that Sid may have been exposed to AIDS. And now we can't have sex for another six months. And we keep talking about getting married and I don't know if I want to be married, but I don't know what else to do because I love him. And he's worried that he's given me AIDS and it's just a horrible mess."

Kathy knelt down next to me and held me tight. "And I'll bet you've been trying to be strong for Sid, too, haven't you?"

"I hope so."

"But this AIDS thing. I thought that was gay men."

"It's transmitted by sexual contact and body fluids, so you can be straight and get it. Sharing needles if you're using drugs. That's how the one girlfriend got it from her boyfriend. Fortunately, that happened after Sid slept with her." I wiped my face, then noticed the tear on my hand, and suddenly pulled away from Kathy. I held up my hand. "Body fluids. Sid and I have been kissing a lot, and it's possible you can get it through saliva."

I explained about the test and that Sid was negative, and why we still had to wait.

"I guess I am worried a little that he has it," I finally said. "Not so much about me. It's just losing him now that he's given up sleeping around. The worst of it is, when we talk about getting married, I want to, and I don't. You know, Kathy, for so long, I've wanted Sid to tell me he loves me, to give up other women, and now that he has, it just feels so weird and scary."

"Small wonder. You two have been fighting your feelings for so long now, it's bound to feel a little strange giving in."

"You think that's it?"

"Well, yes, and a possible deadly disease doesn't help." Kathy looked at me. "How likely is it that Sid picked it up?"

"Not likely at all, for a lot of reasons. Believe me, I've learned a lot more than I ever wanted to about gay sex. Oh, and you cannot get it through casual contact. Hugging is fine. And my tears aren't going through any of your membranes, so you're okay."

"I wasn't worried." Kathy hugged me again. She paused. "You may not want to tell anybody at church, though."

"You're the first person I've told at all. Besides the shrink Sid and I have been seeing. For the trauma."

"Then it's a good thing you are, then."

I cleaned myself up and we went to mass, and after I visited my shut-ins, Kathy and I went to dinner.

But that night, I had two nightmares to Sid's one.

S id, Nick, and I left around nine the next day to get to Mae
and Neil's place. Darby's birthday party was starting early
because the three of us were going to have to leave around
four to get Nick on his flight back to San Jose. That was why
I'd gone to mass the evening before. Sid and I were exhausted,
and I was afraid it showed. He did notice that I'd taken my
dinner ring off.

"Why?" he asked as Nick ran to get his suitcase.

"I just don't want my folks asking awkward questions," I said.

"No. That would not be good."

Sid drove us in his Beemer. As we got onto Interstate 10, he
took a deep breath.

"Nick, Lisa and I have something to tell you," he began.

"Yeah?"

"The problem is you can't tell anybody."

"Oh." He looked really deflated. "I hate secrets."

"It's a good thing, Nick," I said. "We just want to tell you only
because, well..."

"Nick, it looks like Lisa and I will be getting married." Sid
slowed for a car ahead of us, then changed lanes. "We're not
sure when and since Lisa has been getting a lot of pressure
from our friends and her family, we don't want people to know
so that we can make up our own minds."

"Married?" Nick sat up straight. "Does that mean you guys
can take custody of me?"

"Maybe," I said. "We've got a lot to work out. That's why you
can't tell anybody, especially my family."

"Then why are you telling me?"

Sid smiled. "Because after us, you are the one most affected by it. If you can keep this quiet, then maybe you can come and live with us."

Nick made a weird face. "Okay." He sighed and looked out the side window.

Sid and I glanced at each other.

"Does that make you unhappy?" I asked Nick.

"No! I'm happy for you. Really, I am."

Sid looked into his rear-view mirror. "Nick, has somebody else asked you to keep a secret that's not so happy?"

"I'm not being molested, Dad." He rolled his eyes in utter twelve-year-old disdain.

"Honey," I said. "After last year, and Darby's trouble, we have to ask."

"I suppose." He suddenly sat up. "Getting married, huh? You're copping out, Dad."

Sid laughed. "And I'm glad to be. But we don't tell anyone."

"I get it."

When we got to the house, I was a little startled by the "For Sale" sign in the front yard. The lawn had been completely cleared of dead leaves and toys. The rest of the exterior had been freshly painted. Inside, the place sparkled with new paint and an unusual orderliness.

"The kids have been a wonderful help," Mama told me. "It's been a real family project. Even the twins are helping to keep things picked up."

"Have you checked to be sure aliens haven't swapped their bodies or something?" I asked.

Mama laughed.

Nick and Darby ran upstairs to his room and pretty much disappeared until time to eat. After the huge lunch that Mae had made, the party settled down a little. Sid and Mama ended up in the living room. Mae and I landed on the couches in the family room. The kids were all outside in the backyard and relatively quiet, for a change. Possibly because Daddy and Neil were out there, also.

"The place looks great," I told Mae.

"It does. I'm so glad Mama and Daddy have been here. I don't think Neil and I could have done this much in this short a time if they hadn't." Mae giggled. "It's really happening, Lisa. The people at S.C. have been so helpful to Neil. He's going to be able to do research as well as keep up a part-time practice."

"Do you know where you're going to land yet?"

Mae nodded. "I think we're going to end up in Pasadena. There's a school next to Caltech that looks really good. They even have a decent arts program. Apparently, a lot of the Caltech professors send their kids there. Ellen will be so in her own element, and the twins will, too. I'm not sure if we're going to send Darby there. There are a couple of good arts schools nearby, too, so we may go with that option."

"What about Janey?"

"She'll probably end up wherever Darby goes. She's more oriented that way. But there's also an ice rink in Pasadena, so she can keep that up, if she wants to."

"And what about you?"

"I'm thrilled."

"Yeah, but what about making friends and your own life?"

Mae looked at me funny. "I'll be fine. The big problem, of course, is finding someplace we can afford to buy. The good news is Neil has sold his practice."

"Already?"

"Yes. Can you believe it? Which means we'll have even more for a down payment when we sell this place."

"Mommy!" Ellen, in tears, came running in through the sliding glass door. "I fell down!"

Mae scooped her daughter up. "I'm so sorry, sweetie. Let's go see where your boo-boos are."

She took Ellen upstairs.

Feeling... Weird. I ambled to the living room, where Mama and Sid were still talking.

"What's up?" I asked, flopping next to Mama on the couch.

Sid laughed sadly. "Let's just say that your talent for worming things out of me comes honestly."

"What?"

Mama smiled. "We've just been talking about Sid's medical problems right now."

"Really?" I gaped at both of them.

Sid shifted and looked away. Mama smiled.

"I've never heard about this AIDS thing, but it sounds pretty serious," she said.

"He doesn't necessarily have it," I said.

"I know, but you're in limbo." Mama smiled. "Lisle, honey, do you remember when I got breast cancer?"

I groaned. "It was only one of the worst years of my life."

"She was just ten, Sid," Mama said. "My mama came out and went with me and Bill to San Francisco for the surgery and chemotherapy. Bill's mama stayed with the girls."

"That's right," I said. "You had a mastectomy."

"Thought so," Sid said.

"You were checking out my mother's breasts?" I yelped.

"No!" Sid looked a touch frantic. "I, uh, just happened to notice that they didn't always match."

Mama laughed long and hard. "Of course, they don't, honey. Those darned pads always slip." She smiled warmly at Sid. "The important point is that the doctors told me back then, and are still telling me, that the cancer can come back at any time. I have been living for seventeen years with the reality that my cancer will probably come back. That it hasn't has been something of an anomaly, but it's not unheard of, and I'm grateful that it hasn't come back. But every day when I get up, there's always that little thought in the back of my mind. Is today the day I will find that lump? Does this little ache or pain mean that it's here again?"

"How do you live with that?" Sid asked, incredulous.

"I live my life." Mama smiled at him. "I make plans and I go on. I know that cancer may just come along and derail everything. But so can a lot of things. Now, I know you're worried that Lisle could get this thing. And, I am, too. But you didn't want it to happen. You feel really bad that it might. I don't know what Bill will do, but I think you can take him. Sid, honey, the important thing is that you live your life, and you give my baby the best life you can. I trust you to do that."

"I will," said Sid. He took a deep breath. "Without question."

I felt the irritation rise. "I can give myself my own life."

"Lisle, that's not what we meant, and you know it."

"Hmph!"

Sid looked at me and grinned. "Lisa's right, though. She's perfectly capable of managing her own affairs to her liking. I'm just insanely lucky that that those affairs include me."

I felt myself smiling at him. "And you're also insanely lucky that you know what to say at the right time."

Shortly after that, though, we had to collect Nick and head toward LAX. Nick chattered on about his day and the baseball game. Once Nick boarded the plane, I looked at Sid. He shrugged, then turned me toward the parking lot.

"Honestly, Lisa," he said. "Your mother is right about living one day at a time."

"I know. But that she made you responsible for it."

He squeezed my shoulders. "That's just her training. You and I both know that you determine what kind of life you're going to live."

"Hmph!"

Sid laughed and squeezed me again. That night, we both slept through without a nightmare, and I asked him specifically about that the next morning.

"You didn't miss anything, Lisa," Sid told me over breakfast.

I looked at him, suddenly thinking of something. "Sid, it's been over three weeks, hasn't it?"

"What has?" His nose remained buried in the newspaper.

"Since the last time you had sex."

He looked up from the paper. "You're right. It has been."

"You're not feeling grumpy, are you?"

"Not really." He suddenly grinned at me with that hot little smile of his. "Occasionally horny, though."

I laughed and sighed with relief. In fact, we slept through the next night, too. Tuesday night, we did not do as well. Earlier, at Bible Study, Janet Weinstock went into wedding mode and teased me about Sid.

"Everyone knows you're in love with him," Janet announced in front of everybody.

My face flushed and I snarled. "Janet, you're making assumptions you have no right to make!"

I looked around at the shocked faces of the rest of the group, then fled. Esther and Kathy caught me in the parking lot.

"It's okay," Esther said to me. "We know Janet is an idiot."

"And," said Kathy. "She may be making up for something she does not, in fact, have. Lisa, you and Sid are solid. However weird it's feeling right now, I am willing to bet seriously good money that you two are okay."

I squeezed my eyes shut. "I know. We are. But it's still really messed up."

"You two will figure it out," Kathy said.

"And without Janet," Esther added. "What that quote from Shakespeare? The course of true love?"

"Never did run smooth," I finished. "Midsummer's Night Dream. Only my favorite play."

"See?" Esther squeezed my arm. "Then you know it's right."

I let my breath out, then looked at the two of them. "Thank you."

Sadly, their encouragement did not entirely help. When I got home, Sid had already made up the couch in my sewing room.

"You know," I heard myself snarl. "You do not have to assume that I'm going to have a nightmare."

Sid blinked. "What about me?"

"Shavings!" I groaned. "Alright. Fair enough."

I kissed him goodnight with more intensity than I'd planned. And - no surprise - he responded in kind. That we each had a nightmare was no surprise, either.

The next morning, I do not care how much we pretended not to be, we were both a mess. Still, there was work to be done, and we sat next to each other on the couch in my office, going over rejected queries, deciding which ones we'd send to other publications and which ones would end up getting filed.

"Okay, they said they just accepted something on this," I said, showing Sid the last one. "Which means a competing piece."

Sid nodded. "I still like the idea. Why don't we reframe it? I'll write up some options this afternoon."

I think Sid got playful to try and ease the tension and exhaustion we were both feeling. It almost worked. As I made a note on the paper, I noticed that he had a slightly lecherous smile on his face.

"You're staring at my ear." I felt some of the tension ebb a little.

"I'm thinking about how much I want to be nibbling it."

"I'm thinking how much I want you to be nibbling it." I turned and smiled at him. "And a whole lot more."

Sid caught his breath, and I saw my chance to escape. I went over to my desk and dropped the papers on it.

"Lisa, can I ask you a question?" He had a rather puzzled look on his face.

"Sure." I leaned my backside on the desk.

"You've always been very strong on the concept that sex belongs in marriage. And yet, since last summer even, you seem to be okay with us having sex and not waiting."

My insides twisted. "I think it's something Father John told me right after I'd..."

"Yeah." Sid knew I meant right after I'd killed that man.

"I told him it seemed so wrong that I could justify killing someone but not making love to you, who I love. And he said I could justify it. I'm not that rule bound. And I thought about it, and he was right." I looked at him. "I'm not that inflexible. You were bending over backwards trying to be what I needed. I needed to give some. And especially now when we're practically married."

It hit me like a blow to the solar plexus. I burst into tears.

"Lisa." Sid came over and held me. "What is it?"

All I could think was that he'd get afraid again that I was rejecting him. "Sid, no. It's…" I still moved away from him. "Sid, I love you and I'm not going anywhere. I swear to God, I am not. But I really hate the way things are right now. It's so confusing and scary and weird. I just want my old life back. I really do."

"Do you really want to go back to the way things were between us?"

"Yes!" I shrieked, turning away.

Too late I realized what that meant for his life. I heard him leaving the office.

"Sid! No!"

I chased after him and found him in his bedroom, sitting on the edge of his bed.

"Sid, I'm sorry," I said from the doorway. "I know how hard it's been for you to give up fooling around."

"No, you don't." Sid shifted and shook his head. "You don't know because it's actually been pretty damned easy. It's like I said, I've gotten really tired of that scene."

I came over and sat next to him. "I didn't mean what I said like that anyway."

He looked at me, his eyes still hurt. "Are you sure about that?"

I winced. "I don't know. In some ways, maybe I did. Your messing around made you a lot safer for me."

"How?"

"I didn't have to worry about you marrying me." I put my hand on his arm. "I mean, I want to be with you. Absolutely. Don't worry about that part."

He shuddered. "I'll try not to."

"And I really did hate being jealous." I picked at my thumb-nail. "It's just that when I was in the hospital, and you told me you loved me and that you didn't want to sleep around anymore, I was so happy. I was hoping we could be in love, and life would go back to normal, and we could be ourselves and just go on. But now, everything's changing, and we're talking marriage, and I'm scared again."

Sid looked away. "The funny thing is, as I've been sitting here, all I'm thinking is that nothing's changed. We're still not having sex."

I bumped him. "We'll fix that in six months."

"Hopefully. We're still fighting." He sighed. "Somehow, I thought that being in love would mean less of that."

I snorted. "Sid, we've been in love almost since we've known each other, and we've been fighting all along." I flopped onto my back. "We'll be fighting for the rest of our lives."

He looked down at me. "That doesn't bother you?"

"No. Why should it?"

"And being with me for the rest of your life doesn't bother you."

"Sid, I love you." I reached up and touched his chest. "I keep telling you. I want to be with you for the rest of my life. I really do."

"But you're not so excited about getting married."

I winced. "No. I've never wanted to get married. You know that."

Sid slid down onto his side next to me and the bed rocked gently with him. "Lisapet, what is it about marriage that has got you so terrified?"

That took my breath away, but Sid was right. I was flat out scared of getting married.

"I don't know," I said, but then suddenly I did. "I don't want to end up like Mae." I trembled. "She does everything for the kids, Neil, her church, and absolutely nothing for herself.

I mean, in some ways I admire that, but I couldn't be that selfless."

"You can't be selfless? Good lord, Lisa, you put yourself between three kidnappers and their target."

"That just happened. Mae does it day in and day out, and come to think of it, so does Mama. Husband and kids. My entire identity subsumed into that. I don't want that to happen to me and I feel guilty that I'm that selfish."

"Alright, in the first place, I do not want you subsumed into my identity. And in the second..." He sighed. "What Mae does is not healthy. Neil and I were talking about it last Sunday. He's getting worried about her."

"It's what's expected of me."

"So what?"

"There's just a lot of pressure out there. Ann Landers insisting that toddlers be watched every second. Magazine articles on what makes a good mom, and putting your children first, and still keeping your husband part of it. Having It All."

"That was a wretched book. Okay, so there are societal norms to deal with. We will."

"You're not the one who's expected to change her name."

"You're right. But I do get to be the one to remind you that whatever we do, we do on our terms, not on anyone else's." He smiled at me. "One thing you and I have in common is that we both, each in our own way, love to buck societal norms. And we both work within them, when necessary. It's why I wear clothes."

I laughed. Sid is a nudist at heart, although he is also a clotheshorse.

"I guess. The problem is, I sort of want to get married. I do like the sacramental part of it. That's important to me."

"I think I get that." Sid's hand gently brushed my cheek. "Either way, you and I will decide how marriage will work for us or even if marriage will work for us."

"But I promised—"

"You didn't promise to marry me. You asked if we could. In a fit of euphoria, I might add." His hand cupped my chin. "What you did promise is to be with me and that's all I care about."

"It's all I care about. Being with you, I mean." I blinked. "I love you so much, Sid."

"And I love you, Lisa."

He kissed me, softly at first, then more deeply as he slid halfway on top of me. I sighed as I reached for more, but then Sid pulled away and sat up.

"What did I do?" I sniffed anxiously.

"Oh, nothing much." His smile took on a rueful cast as he pulled me upright. "Just made me really wish that we could make love." He sighed deeply, got up, then bent over and kissed me. "My sweet Lisa, I can't tell you how much I want you in my bed."

"And I can't tell you how much I'm looking forward to being there." As I got to my feet, I looked around. "Sid, when the time comes, which bedroom are we going to move into?"

He started to answer, then looked around, himself. "I guess I have been assuming you'll move in here."

"So have I." I winced. "It still feels like your bedroom, though."

"I know. And you have your bedroom." He shook his head. "I wonder if that's what we need. A new place, someplace that will truly be ours. I mean, that's been the problem, hasn't it? We're trying to figure out who we are as a couple, and what a lifetime commitment to each other is going to look like. So, why not start with where we live?"

"I suppose." I frowned. "But I don't understand how that will make it easier to figure out who we are as a couple."

He looked around the room again, with its dark cherry wood dresser and headboard, the sliding mirrored doors to the closet, and dark brown drapes with off-white sheers underneath covering the sliding glass doors to the side yard and the hot tub.

"I'm not sure either, except that no matter how much I remind myself that this house is technically ours, I keep thinking of it as my house." His arm slid across my shoulder. "This is my room, my private territory, and you have your room and your private territory. And this is my bed, not ours. I think we need a place that is truly ours."

"That makes sense." I made a face. "But I like this place. It's got a lot of good memories."

Sid gave me a quick squeeze. "Yeah. It does. Why don't we look around anyway? See what's out there."

"I don't want to move too far away. Church, you know."

"That is where our friends are." He steered me into the hall. "Why don't you go tell Conchetta that we're going to eat lunch out again and I'll call a couple real estate agents and make some appointments."

I stopped at the end of the hall. "What about getting married?"

He smiled. "We'll take that one off the table for the time being. If we decide to get married, we can do it at any time. In the meantime, we'll just be us."

"That sounds good." I frowned. "So, what do we call us?"

"We're partners." He grinned.

"They're going to call us boyfriend and girlfriend."

"Let 'em."

I smiled. "I'm going to go put my dinner ring on."

April 18-20, 1985

I t was Thursday and another meeting with Dr. Heilland. I was really nervous on the way over. But after my nightmare that night, Sid and I agreed it was time to talk about the kidnapping. In the session, we did mention the fight the day before, that had probably been triggered by the trauma, and that it was time to do something about it.

"Alright," said Dr. Heilland. "Remember, this is about de-sensitizing you to the trauma. This is why relaxation and remembering that this is a safe place is very important. I want you both to get good and relaxed and to remember that you are in a safe place."

So, Sid and I closed our eyes and held hands, and I told them about what had happened.

I'd wakened up in the room feeling nauseous. As I spewed onto the floor, I realized that I'd been sedated. A man in black fatigues watched, then shoved me back onto the rickety metal bed with the thin mattress and squeaky springs. My ankle wore a manacle, and I was chained to the bed. I had a piece of spring steel in my hair - Sid says you can always hide something. But with the man watching me I couldn't use it.

He cleaned up the mess I'd made without a word. The room was roughly paneled in wood and looked unfinished. Light came from the window above the bed. I was scared and let myself act scared. I didn't want him to think I was an operative. And then I was cold, and I was glad I still had a sweater on and socks. I didn't know where my shoes were.

For those first couple, three days, I was watched constantly. I couldn't even go to the bathroom without them watching, which was really embarrassing. All I had was a can to go in, but it was cleaned after every time I used it. I could tell from the sounds of the voices in the other room that there were four of them total. They switched off watching me, but at least one was always watching me until... It must have been Sunday night. That's when I scratched a signal for Sid into the wall. Proverbs Twenty-Seven Fourteen: "He that greets his brother with a loud voice in the morning, a curse shall be laid to his charge." It's my favorite verse. I'm not a morning person and Sid is.

I was so scared the entire time. I had my nightmare about the first kill every time I went to sleep. But I was bored, too. The men all spoke Spanish, although one did speak a little English. But he wouldn't talk to me at all. I did look out the window, and all there was around me was desert scrub. I wondered where I was. Sometimes, I could hear one of them leave in the black van I saw out the window.

Finally, two of them came into the room. They handcuffed me in front of myself, then unchained my leg, and dragged me to the other room. There was a phone on the table. My shoes were on a kitchen counter behind me.

"Call your husband," the one man ordered.

"I'm not married," I squeaked.

"Call your boyfriend, then. We've seen him before."

I picked up the receiver, then dialed Sid's personal line. Then the receiver was ripped from my hands. The man made his demand and my heart pounded when he mentioned Eliana Martinez. I didn't want them to trade that sweet girl for me, but I also wanted to go home.

The man put the receiver to my ear and mouth.

"Hi," I said. "I'm scared.

"Are they treating you okay?" It was Sid's voice, and I was so glad to hear it.

"Yeah. But I'm scared. I'm really scared."

"It's okay. They're all praying for you here. Be strong, honey. I—"

The receiver was ripped away. Then the two men pushed me back into the room and chained me back to the bed. They'd said Wednesday.

With at least three of them in the other room, I didn't think I could take them. So, it was back to waiting. Then, the next morning, there was an argument of some kind. I saw three of them getting into the van and could hear the fourth pacing in the next room. It was the best chance I'd had.

I got my spring steel out of my hair, popped the lock on the manacle, and got the other end open and off the bed. Then I waited. The other man eventually came into the room. He was so startled when I rushed him that I was able to whack him in the head with the manacle chain, and he sank to his knees. I ran from the room, locked the door behind me, then looked for my shoes. Given the scrub outside, I was not going to get very far in stocking feet. The shoes were still on the counter, and I got them on as fast as I could. I also found a canteen and filled it with water from the kitchen sink.

Then I slid outside and ran. I stayed to the scrub, heading south and down the hills. You can usually find people that way, although I had no idea how far I'd have to go. I don't know how long I'd been running when I first saw the chopper heading toward where I'd been held. It was coming from the west and flew over where the house was, then circled back, coming closer to me, and I saw the LASD on the side. I tried waving, but it went on. So, I went back to running. It did come back, circling over where the house was, then further and further out. I waved again, and it flew over right on top of me. The loudspeaker asked if I was okay, and I gave them the thumbs up. They told me to stay put, that the Forest Service paramedics would be there soon. Then a red chopper flew up and landed nearby, and the guys came running out with a board, got me loaded up and away we went.

Dr. Heilland smiled. "You did that very well. How are you feeling?"

I took a deep breath. "A little shaky, but okay."

Sid chuckled. "I think you were more traumatized by the idea of marrying me than you were by the kidnapping."

"But the kidnapping changed everything, Sid. That's when you said you loved me."

"Sid, how are you feeling?" Dr. Heilland asked.

"A little shaky, I guess. It was a pretty rough five days." He looked at me, then put his arm around me. "I also feel immensely proud of you, Lisa. You did everything just right."

Dr. Heilland tapped his pen on his notepad. "Lisa, you said you had nightmares while you were held?"

"Just the one. I keep having it. My first kill. It happened last summer."

"With your values, I can imagine you're having trouble with it." He sighed. "However, we are out of time. Will I see you two next week?"

"Sure," I said.

"Yeah," said Sid.

Outside the office, our pagers went off. We both groaned.

"My turn to call, I think." I said.

We went to a coffee shop near the office, and Sid watched me fondly as I dialed in, got the receiver code and our orders.

"Well?" he asked.

"We've got an evidence swap tonight. Turns out Mr. Danschenko is hiding out in his warehouse after all. FBI will be raiding at twenty-three-thirty. We've got to get in and out of the office by twenty-three hundred. Oh, and one more fun little piece. If we could just happen to get Danschenko trussed and ready to go, that would be good."

Sid made a face. Evidence swaps were tricky. The job was to slip in, find a piece of evidence that was highly classified, then exchange it for other evidence that wasn't quite so sensitive. That wasn't so hard. That the places we were breaking into often had people in them who neither wanted to be arrested, nor wanted us to get the evidence, that was the hard part.

"Well, at least we know the layout," he said, finally. "Back to house hunting?"

"Sure."

As the afternoon wore on, though, we didn't see anything that excited or interested us. Sid wanted plenty of bedrooms for when Mae, Neil, and the kids visited. We needed office space. I wanted a big front window to put a Christmas tree in. We both thought a more open layout would be good for when we did entertain, although we did want to keep a library room. I needed a sewing room, too.

We got home in time for dinner, then went to work on all the stuff we should have been working on that afternoon. I was typing away at the computer when I sat back to consider my next line and looked around. I liked my office, with its dark paneling and the photos I'd hung on the wall. I did think I might want the walls a little lighter, maybe nice floral upholstery on the couch.

I got up and went into Sid's office. He looked up from his computer.

"Yes?" he asked.

"I just had an idea." I flopped into one of the chairs in front of his desk. "Did you see anything yesterday or today that looked even remotely workable?"

"Not a damn thing." He looked at me and frowned. "We've only been looking for two days, though."

"I like this place," I said. I looked around. His office could use some lightening up, too. "Do you think if we redecorated, maybe did some remodeling, we could make it ours enough?"

Sid sat back. "That's a good idea."

"You don't mind having your home remade?"

"Nah." Sid smiled. "Frankly, this was just the first place that looked livable when I was assigned here. Any attachment I have to it is what you've brought to it."

"Okay. I guess we just have to find a contractor now." I checked my watch. "And we've got to get into our break-in clothes."

"Meet you at the garage door in fifteen."

We took my truck that night. Danschenko had seen Sid's Beemer. We wore black pants with lots of extra pockets and loaded down with tools. Our black zip-front sweatshirts were in the jump seat behind us with black leather gloves and all-over ski masks tucked into the pockets, and we both had light-colored shirts on. It was a little after ten when I parked on the street just outside the industrial park. Fortunately, mine wasn't the only vehicle around. Sid and I got our sweat-shirts on, then did a quick walk around the building were Danschenko's office was. There were lights on over every door, but no video cameras. I knew from our orders that an armed security guard patrolled the buildings every other hour, and that he would have just passed. After getting our gloves and masks on, we squeezed behind the shrubbery next to the boarded-up front door of the office and peeked in. We could see the faint glow of a light coming from the main office, but not where, exactly, the light was.

We went around to the back door. Sid had the locks picked in several minutes. I pulled my gun from the holster in the back of my waistband. Sid opened the door very softly and slowly. I rolled in. The warehouse was mostly dark, with weak lights at the tops of the shelves. I listened. There was no sound of movement.

"Clear," I hissed, and Sid slid in behind me, shutting the door. I crept along the wall toward the packing station, then grinned when I saw something lying on the counter. A roll of strapping tape. I showed Sid and he nodded. We made our way along the front of the warehouse to the door into the main office. I put my ear to the door and listened. Someone on the other side was humming something mournful and pacing.

"Now what?" I asked Sid.

"Wait a few."

Sure enough, the humming and pacing faded behind the sound of a door closing. Sid checked the door. It was locked. I kept listening as Sid went to work. He looked up at me and nodded, his blue eyes twinkling in the dim light. Again, I went to the side of the door that opened, and got my gun braced. Sid slowly opened it. I rolled in.

The main office was dark, but a light glowed under the closed door to Danschenko's office. The other back-office door was open and there was no one inside. Sid slid in behind me and silently shut the door. We could hear the faint humming from Danschenko's office. Sid pointed to the front of the secretary's desk, and I nodded. He got some pencils from the top. I crouched behind him in front of the desk. Sid tossed one of the pencils at the door to the warehouse. The humming abruptly stopped. Sid tossed a second one. The door to the inner office slowly creaked open. Danschenko, carrying an automatic pistol, slid out of the office, then cautiously up to the door to the warehouse. He turned and walked straight toward Sid and me, but his eyes were on the door to the foyer. I held my breath.

He had just gone past us when Sid pounced on his back and knocked him to the ground. I scooted the automatic Danschenko had been carrying out of the way as Danschenko struggled. He rolled on top of Sid and drew his hand back to punch him, but I caught it and yanked it further behind him.

Danschenko howled in pain, still he did not give up struggling. Sid punched him in the jaw, then rolled out from underneath him. I still had Danschenko's hand, and was about to lose my grip, when Sid kneed him in the belly. Danschenko fell on his face, and Sid got his knee in Danschenko's back. I had the tape out in an instant, whipping it around Danschenko's wrists as Sid held them up for me. A couple minutes later, we had Danschenko's feet and left him hog-tied in front of the desk.

We were breathing heavily when we hurried to the inner office and started going through it. I searched the desk and credenza while Sid went through the files. We didn't care about it being messy. The FBI wouldn't mind.

"Got it," Sid hissed. I handed him the substitute evidence, then hurried out to the front office. Danschenko was struggling and the tape on his wrist strained. I whipped some more tape around him, then turned. Sid was rummaging through the refrigerator. He palmed something into the pocket on his leg as I yanked him to the warehouse door. We slid along the wall, but we could hear tires rolling across the pavement outside. Underneath the crack between the roll-up door and the ground, we saw the glare of red and blue lights. The Feds were there.

Sid nodded at the ladder to the roof. I went up first, and then he did.

"Federal agents!" growled a voice through a speaker. "Open up or we're coming in."

We peeked over the edge of the roof. The agents were focused on both the front and back doors. Sid nodded at the far end of the building. We'd seen a ladder there, too. Keeping low and moving softly, we hurried to that end and scrambled down the ladder, jumping when the ladder stopped about seven feet above the ground. We made our way around the side of another building, then hurried toward my truck. Somebody must have seen something, because as we were about to get in, we saw flashlights coming our way. Sid slid into the passenger seat.

"Wanna neck?" Sid gasped as he got his mask, gloves, and sweatshirt off, and I got in and shut the door.

"Yeah." I pulled off my mask, gloves, and sweatshirt, too.

Sid's eyes gleamed with mischief. "On my lap?"

I giggled, wriggled myself around so that I would face him and carefully slid onto his lap. The windows were getting nice and foggy as Sid moaned and I kissed him and moaned also. The truck rocked rhythmically.

"I could have sworn they went this way," someone snarled.

A beam of light flashed through the windows.

"Oh, yeah. Oh, keep it going!" I cried.

The men cursed and the flashlights retreated. As soon as we were sure they were gone, Sid gave me one last kiss, then burst into laughter as I maneuvered myself around the gear shift and into the driver's seat.

"Did I do that right?" I asked, blushing a little.

"Yes!" He laughed even harder. "Where did you learn that?"

"One of your girlfriends last spring. You two were doing it in the living room and I happened to go into the hall. I did not go any further."

"I'm sorry about that." He sighed.

I shrugged and started the engine. "Sid, I can't worry about what all you did." I slowly pulled the truck down the road away from the flashing lights and black cars. "And in some ways, I may even want to be grateful. As Angelique once put it, I will eventually reap the benefit of your antics. Speaking of, how are you feeling?"

"Ohhhh." Sid laughed. "Pretty keyed up."

I sighed. "I guess I'm sleeping in my own bed tonight."

"I'm afraid so, honey." He sighed deeply. "Yeah, we could be having some fun right now."

"October, right?"

"Hopefully." He slid his hand along the inside of my thigh.

"Sid. I'm trying to drive and that's not helping."

"We'll figure something out. And, by the way. I got some." He held up two of the flat jars with the blue lid.

"You stole some beluga!"

"Who's going to notice? And it's the best caviar in the world."

We both slept through the night, and the next morning, Sid showed me the file he'd found: Danschenko's notes on my kidnapping and the CIA's and the Colombians' involvement in it. Turns out Danschenko had agreed to help the cartel get Eliana in exchange for the cartel taking out a target that the CIA wanted taken care of.

"Good lord. He was sucking up to everybody." I grumbled.

"Looks like," Sid said.

We never did find out what happened to Danschenko.

I didn't have too much time to complain about it, though. It was the day before Kathy and Jesse's wedding. Frank had twisted Sid's arm into playing the organ for them and dragged Sid to the church to practice. The rehearsal dinner was a little tense, but that was just nerves and the fact that Kathy and Estelle's parents were all but estranged from their daughters.

Then it was the big day. Sid and I were thrilled that we had again slept through the night without any nightmares. The wedding, itself, was gorgeous, and we ended up having a blast at the reception. Sid and Esther turned the air blue at our table, trying to one up each other with dirty innuendos. Janet and Sylvia saw us dancing together and smirked. Then Sylvia had to ask when we were getting married.

I just grinned. "Maybe we already are."

Both their faces fell.

"Or maybe we won't get married at all," said Sid.

"You know, I just heard about a Celtic sexual initiation ritual," I said. "We should think about that."

Janet and Sylvia backed away. Sid laughed, but I was a little disappointed. We'd come up with about five or six scenarios that all avoided a wedding, each more ridiculous than the one before. I'd really wanted to see the look on Janet's face when we told her we'd gone to Las Vegas and gotten married by an Elvis impersonator.

We sent Kathy and Jesse on their honeymoon, then Sid and I went home. He made toast points from good French bread and served them with icy, cold vodka and some of the beluga caviar he'd taken from Danschenko's refrigerator. And I finally opened my birthday presents.

Coming Soon

Book Eight in the Operation Quickline series *A Little Family Business*

Life changes at the speed of light

After Lisa makes a disastrous pickup for Operation Quickline, the top-secret courier group that she and her partner Sid Hackbirn work for, she realizes it's time for her and Sid to get married. They're already re-building their house and have merged their assets. Sid's given up sleeping around.

But then the two have to take custody of Sid's son, Nick, after the boy's mother dies. Suddenly becoming full-time parents to an almost adolescent is hard enough. There's also getting a grieving and clingy Nick settled, planning a wedding with Lisa's mother intent on going hog-wild, and even finding someone to take care of the pets. Sid's and Lisa's lives have gotten far more complicated than either imagined.

And that's not counting their little side business. Thanks to the bad pickup, Sid and Lisa are ordered to find a missing operative and get embroiled in an arms-trading scheme. Worse yet, Nick figures out all too quickly that his dad and Lisa don't have a normal job, and it's not long before the spy business becomes a family thing, assuming they all can stay alive long enough.

Other books by Anne Louise Bannon

I'm so glad you liked this book! Check out my other novels, available in print or ebook at your favorite retailer:

Freddie and Kathy Series:
Fascinating Rhythm
Bring Into Bondage
The Last Witnesses
Blood Red

Operation Quickline Series
That Old Cloak and Dagger Routine
Stopleak
Deceptive Appearances
Fugue in a Minor Key
Sad Lisa
These Hallowed Halls
My Sweet Lisa

Old Los Angeles
Death of the Zanjero
Death of the City Marshal
Death of the Chinese Field Hands
Death of an Heiress

Daria Barnes
Rage Issues

Mrs. Sperling
A Nose for a Niedeman

Brenda Finnegan
Tyger, Tyger

Romantic Fiction
White House Rhapsody, Book One and Two

Fantasy and Science Fiction
A Ring for a Second Chance
But World Enough and Time

And I would be honored if you left a review for this and any
of my books on GoodReads or any other retail site. It really
helps.

Connect with Anne Louise Bannon

Thank you for sticking it out this long! Please join my newsletter. It's the best way to stay up-to-date on my upcoming projects, blog posts and even games and giveaways.

Sign up here: http://eepurl.com/zH0Ab

Or connect with me on your favorite social media platforms:

Visit my website: http://annelouisebannon.com

Friend me on Facebook: http://facebook.com/RobinGoodfellowEnt

Follow me on Twitter: http://twitter.com/ALBannon

Favorite my Smashwords author page: https://www.smashwords.com/profile/view/MsBriscow

Connect on LinkedIn: http://www.linkedin.com/in/annelouisebannon

Follow me on Pinterest: http://pinterest.com/msbriscow

About Anne Louise Bannon

Anne Louise Bannon is an author and journalist who wrote her first novel at age 15. Her journalistic work has appeared in Ladies' Home Journal, the Los Angeles Times, Wines and Vines, and in newspapers across the country. She was a TV critic for over 10 years, founded the YourFamilyViewer blog, and created the OddBallGrape.com wine education blog with her husband, Michael Holland. She is the co-author of How-dunit: Book of Poisons, with Serita Stevens, as well as author of the Freddie and Kathy mystery series, set in the 1920s, the Old Los Angeles series, set in 1870, and the Operation Quick-line series, plus several stand alones. She and her husband live in Southern California with an assortment of critters.